LETTERS FROM THE GROUND TO THE HEART

LETTERS FROM THE GROUND TO THE HEART

Beauty Amid Destruction

ANNE THOMAS

FOREWORD BY BRIAN PENRY

ANNE IN JAPAN PUBLISHING · 2011

ANNE IN JAPAN

Published by Anne In Japan Publishing, USA
First Edition – December 2011
Copyright ©2011 by Anne Thomas. All Rights Reserved.
Edited by Brian Penry. Foreword by the Editor.
Library of Congress Control Number: 2011916623
ISBN 978-1-257-90208-8

www.lettersfromthegroundtotheheart.com

GRATEFUL ACKNOWLEDGEMENTS

Dorian de Wind & The Huffington Post
The Moderate Voice · Ode Magazine & www.odewire.com
The Sydney Morning Herald, Sydney, Australia
The Block Island Times

Dusk on the River from *Start Where You Are,* by Pema Chödrön.
©1994 by Pema Chödrön. Reprinted by arrangement with
Shambhala Publications Inc., Boston, MA

Ame Ni Mo Makezu (Be not Defeated by the Rain) by Miyazawa Kenji (1896-1933).
Translation by David Sulz, Edmonton, Alberta, Canada

The many, kind respondents to Anne's letters from the world over

The *'Letters'* Team – Katie Keenan, Sue Brown Black, Elliot Taubman,
Mark & Alisa Mierzejewski (USA); Chella Ramanan, Rachel Castagne (UK)

Our host non profit organization, Block Island Ecumenical Ministries (BIEM), Inc.

Henry "Had" Brown (1915-2009)

Jacket & Text Design by Brian Penry
Thanks to Jane Sheppard & Thomas Cahill

Cover photo of cherry blossoms in Japan by Zuki Harahap · Jakarta, Indonesia
Taken shortly after the Tohoku (aka) Great East Japan Earthquake and Tsunami

Back Cover Photo of Anne Thomas courtesy of Sendai Yomawari Group, Sendai Japan

English text set in Garamond & Trajan Pro | Japanese text set in Hiragino Kaku Gothic

Printed & distributed by the global network of Lulu Enterprises, Inc. · www.lulu.com

PUBLISHER'S NOTE

LETTERS FROM THE GROUND TO THE HEART

CONTENTS

THE RESPONSES

PAST PERFECT

HOW TO HELP   *211*

ACKNOWLEDGEMENTS   *213*

ABOUT THE AUTHOR   *215*

With the deepest of Love and admiration
I dedicate this book to the Japanese people,
thanking them for manifesting the very best
that we humans can be.

FOREWORD

It was Sunday, March 13, 2011, two days after a massive, 9.0 magnitude earthquake and tsunami struck the Northeastern Region of Japan known as Tohoku. While sipping coffee and going through e-mails as is my early morning ritual, I noticed an excerpt from a blog post at odemagazine.com (now odewire.com) that a friend in the UK had sent me. It was the first of what would become a series of accounts of life in Sendai, Japan following these terrible events, the ramifications of which were then and are yet unfolding – written by an American woman who has lived there for some time.

However and rather than being predictably consumed with the statistics of death and destruction, the sum effect of her account was as though "reading" a Van Gogh painting. The words that floated up off my screen spoke of "the heavens at night" being "scattered with stars," life in Sendai being "surreal", and the "enormous Cosmic evolutionary step that is occurring all over the world right at this moment." These were no ordinary thoughts – certainly not those of one processing the aftermath of tragic events in ordinary ways.

I was moved to print this out and read it aloud at a time of sharing during church services, later that morning. It bears mentioning that I have never been very keen on organized religion, attending services only very rarely in recent years, at a white clapboard, 1700s era New England church, with a small, closely knit congregation. You could hear a pin drop as I read it, at times tearfully – to a similar response. I was still hearing from other congregants, weeks after. It was only later in the course of this project, that I would learn that this very same experience was not unique to me.

I searched online for this person who signed her posts at the time simply as "Anne in Japan." I found one Anne Thomas, a U.S.-born professor of English, who after living for years throughout the world, had settled in Sendai – where she has taught at various university positions and made her home for over twenty-two years.

I quickly became transfixed by Anne's posts, each an elegant yet spare homage to the simple virtues of a people and culture that has been through incredible natural, as well as unnatural disasters – not once, but many times – somehow not merely rebounding, but thriving after each, brutal challenge to their very being.

It wasn't long before I found myself reaching out to Anne, who graciously added me to her e-mail list. We began corresponding, and I suggested soon thereafter that we collect her letters in a book. The purpose is twofold: to give her work a greater voice and audience, while raising funds to help survivors of the earthquake and tsunami. Perhaps notably, it is not these events themselves that precipitated her letters; it is the countless acts of human grace that followed – and which continue to inspire Anne, and all who read her words.

As though modest gifts in small, neatly lacquered Japanese boxes, each letter is a tiny gem. Like one in a set of Russian Matryoshka dolls, each is its own story unto itself – while fitting perfectly inside the next to create a larger story.

Through Anne, one vicariously witnesses a quietly dignified, orderly response to utter and complete chaos which, vs. the physical (cherry blossoms) is the true essence of "Beauty Amid Destruction." Anne's letters offer simple, unadorned accounts, often of the most mundane tasks – however, in ways that make fascinating the stories of people trying to function normally in the most abnormal of circumstances. They are at once a transformational tale – an illuminating journey to a greater, universally shared consciousness.

As you peruse the tiny sampling of responses that Anne has received from every corner of the world, you will find that I am far from alone in these observations. From New Zealand, Australia, Holland and the United Arab Emirates to France, Brazil and throughout the U.S. and beyond, Anne taps into our collective empathy – resonating with people of every conceivable age, background and persuasion. Ranging from simple messages of support to extraordinary perspectives, first-hand accounts and the aid-related initiatives of others, the responses include those of Anne's family, friends, students past and present, and notably a gentleman named Imai Sensei, whom Anne reveres in great part for his many years and tireless efforts on behalf of Japan's homeless – whom recent events have tested as never before.

This effort closes with excerpts from a letter of another time, which was included at the suggestion of Anne's cousin, Susan Brown Black, who has also contributed to this effort in profound ways. It was written by their late uncle, Henry "Had" Brown over the course of several days in October, 1945. Ironically, Had also chronicled events in and around the environs of Sendai to family and friends following disaster, albeit manmade rather than natural – while on leave as a U.S. military officer at the close of World War II.

It is doubly ironic, if not uncanny that the observations of Anne and her Uncle Had bracket the exact period of time during which nuclear events forever changed, and are yet again reshaping both Japan and our entire world. However and rather than delving into such bleak matters, their writings ultimately offer the prospect of hope.

Where Anne focuses more on the people of Japan, Had was clearly fascinated by its beauty and culture. And while each writes from distinctly different vantage points, their two perspectives are separated only by time and circumstances. Both reveal one, consummate and powerfully enduring truth: that the timeless, mystical nature of Japan is inextricably intertwined with the kind spirit, patience and generosity of its people – call it their 'cultural fortitude,' which the Japanese seem somehow hardwired to share not only with each other, but especially and *instinctively* in times of extreme challenge with those around them, as well.

A few thoughts in closing…

I ask that you please keep Anne's observations in their full context. Her positive, upbeat appraisals of efforts to rebuild should not be misconstrued to mean that the immediacy and urgency of Japan's needs has somehow past. *Many, particularly in Tohoku, the Northeastern Region of Japan – are yet in dire need of assistance.*

Lastly, my hope is that through these collected letters and more, that Anne's message, along with those of others will now reach, enlighten and inspire larger, more diverse audiences – perhaps to think differently, more compassionately about people and cultures other than their own – and above all, *to act* – not only in times of need, but through small acts of kindness, throughout the precious moments of each day.

– Brian Penry

TEN LESSONS
FROM
THE JAPANESE

TEN LESSONS FROM THE JAPANESE – WHAT CAN WE LEARN?

The world can learn much from The Japanese – as they patiently and ably bear the brunt of Nature's fury after the earthquake and tsunami, as a result of their precarious location on the Ring of Fire.*

*Volcanoes, Fault Lines, Tectonic Plate Edge.

I

CALM

Not a single visual of chest-beating or wild grief.
Sorrow itself has been elevated.

II

DIGNITY

Disciplined queues for water and groceries.
Not a rough word or crude gesture.

III

ABILITY

The incredible architects, for but one example.
Buildings swayed but most did not fall.

IV

GRACE

People bought only what they needed for the present, so everybody could get something.

V

ORDER

Almost no looting.
No honking and no overtaking on the roads – just understanding.

VI

SACRIFICE

Fifty workers stayed back to pump sea water in the nuclear reactors.
How will they ever be repaid?

VII

TENDERNESS

Restaurants cut prices. An unguarded ATM was left alone.
The strong cared for the weak.

VIII

TRAINING

The old and the children, everyone knew exactly what to do –
and they did just that.

IX

MEDIA

The media showed magnificent restraint in their bulletins – no silly
reporters, only calm reportage.

X

CONSCIENCE

When the power went off in a store, people put things back on the
shelves and left quietly.

Can we share these virtues with our Children, Family and Friends in
their respective positions and professions?

This courtesy of sharing valuable information might go a long way in
reminding people of the Path of Propriety.

THE
LETTERS

LETTER ONE · BLESSINGS

March 13, 2011

Hello My Lovely Family and Friends,

First I want to thank you so very much for your concern for me. I am very touched. I also wish to apologize for a generic message to you all. But it seems the best way at the moment to get my message to you.

Things here in Sendai have been rather surreal. But I am very blessed to have wonderful friends who are helping me a lot. Since my shack is even more worthy of that name, I am now staying at a friend's home. We share supplies like water, food and a kerosene heater. We sleep lined up in one room, eat by candlelight, share stories. It is warm, friendly, and beautiful.

During the day we help each other clean up the mess in our homes. People sit in their cars, looking at news on their navigation screens, or line up to get drinking water when a source is open. If someone has water running in their home, they put out sign so people can come to fill up their jugs and buckets.

Utterly amazingly where I am there has been no looting, no pushing in lines. People leave their front door open, as it is safer when an earthquake strikes. People keep saying, "Oh, this is how it used to be in the old days when everyone helped one another."

Quakes keep coming. Last night they struck about every 15 minutes. Sirens are constant and helicopters pass overhead often.

We got water for a few hours in our homes last night, and now it is for half a day. Electricity came on this afternoon. Gas has not yet come on. But all of this is by area. Some people have these things, others do not. No one has washed for several days. We feel grubby, but there are so much more important concerns than that for us now. I love this peeling away of non-essentials. Living fully on the level of instinct, of intuition, of caring, of what is needed for survival, not just of me, but of the entire group.

There are strange parallel universes happening. Houses a mess in some places, yet then a house with futons or laundry out drying in the sun. People lining up for water and food, and yet a few people out walking   their dogs. All happening at the same time.

Other unexpected touches of beauty are first, the silence at night. No cars. No one out on the streets. And the heavens at night are scattered with stars. I usually can see about two, but now the whole sky is filled. The mountains around Sendai are solid and with the crisp air we can see them silhouetted against the sky magnificently.

And the Japanese themselves are so wonderful. I come back to my shack to check on it each day, now to send this e-mail since the electricity is on, and I find food and water left in my entranceway. I have no idea from whom, but it is there. Old men in green hats go from door to door checking to see if everyone is OK. People talk to complete strangers asking if they need help. I see no signs of fear. Resignation, yes, but fear or panic, no.

They tell us we can expect aftershocks, and even other major quakes, for another month or more. And we are getting constant tremors, rolls, shaking, rumbling. I am blessed in that I live in a part of Sendai that is a bit elevated, a bit more solid than other parts. So, so far this area is better off than others. Last night my friend's husband came in from the country, bringing food and water. Blessed again.

Somehow at this time I realize from direct experience that there is indeed an enormous Cosmic evolutionary step that is occurring all over the world right at this moment. And somehow as I experience the events happening now in Japan, I can feel my heart opening very wide. My brother asked me if I felt so small because of all that is happening. I don't. Rather, I feel as though part of something happening that is much larger than myself. This wave of birthing (worldwide) is hard, and yet magnificent.

Thank you again for your care and Love of me.

With Love in return, to you all,

Anne

LETTER TWO

March 16, 2011

Dear Family and Friends,

Once again I want to write to you about what is happening here. The TV news is frightening beyond belief. In fact, this entire phenomenon seems totally surreal. Beyond the edges of one's wildest imagination. But I continue picking through the rubble of this experience to find flickers of hope and powerful experiences of beauty.

Yes, the devastation continues, as do deep concerns over the nuclear fallout. But along side of the ongoing horrific news we have started hearing stories of a positive nature. They may be small and subtle, but they are emerging. A doctor, for example, who lost his home and clinic, went to live in an evacuee shelter. He immediately saw the tremendous medical needs there, so began treating patients to the best of his ability. A nurse came in by helicopter to offer her services. During her interview she said, "People must overcome this crisis. We cannot give up."

Likewise a restaurant owner, who also lost his home, but not his business, opened up shop and offered hot bowls of noodle soup to evacuees for free. "We must help one another," was his only comment.

Indeed, a friend in Tokyo wrote this to me in an e-mail:

"I know that all Japanese people can exercise their best to help others in such serious circumstances and you can rely on their kindness. That is our culture. Of course, I am ready to support you with anything you need, so please don't hesitate, but let me know whatever I can do to support you."

In evacuation centers there are puppet shows for children. "It's to ease their minds," my friend explained to me. "That is very important." And for the Japanese one's state of mind often carries more weight than facts. That is because we have some semblance of control over one's mind, no matter what the outer circumstances may be.

In another shelter junior high school students got paper and paints and made a large bright, energetic sign that said, "To have life is profound joy." It was hung high overhead so everyone could see it and be encouraged by the words.

On local TV stations time is allotted to read messages of people seeking family members. We comfort one another as best as we can. We still say, "Gambarimashou" (We must keep up our fighting spirit). We see shots on TV of family members reuniting, of long lines of people waiting to use free phone service to call home and friends. We see a lot of tears. But so much comfort, so much support.

The city's basic infrastructure has collapsed, but people are working round the clock to get things back into some sort of normalcy. Water came first in big trucks. Then in some areas it was on after a day. Electricity is also slowly coming back on. Gas will not be available for another month or so because of excessive damage to the pipes. We are all dreaming of a bath, of just being able to wash a bit. But as one woman in a shelter said, "I was so cold at night, but everyone else was, too. So, that gives me courage." In that context a bath seems so minor.

Buses have resumed on some routes. Some food shops are open for a few hours a day. I noticed a shop open with flowers for graves, for shrines and temples so that the souls of the long ago and recently deceased may have a touch of earthly beauty in heaven.

There is so much support and solidarity. I want to close with another e-mail from a friend who is a university teacher. It, too, is an excellent manifestation of the truly remarkable Japanese "kokoro" (heart and soul).

. . .

"I have been trying to find out the situations of some students and friends whom I lost contact with since the earthquake and tsunami attacked this area.

"There are still many students staying and living on campus. Some lost their houses and the others are not sure if their families are OK. When I met them, I just couldn't find right word to cheer them up.

"Today was supposed to be a graduation day which was postponed and might be canceled. When I saw the students at the campus housing this morning, they served me a special breakfast that the juniors cooked for the seniors to celebrate the day. The meal was cold, but really special. I won't forget the taste of it. I am convinced that my students will overcome this tragedy with a positive attitude. I intend to emulate them."

. . .

With Love,

Anne

LETTER THREE

March 18, 2011 (early)

Dear Friends and Family,

Life here has become one of living day to day. I am staying with the mother of my best friend, Izumi. Her home is two minutes from my unlivable shack. Izumi has moved in there, too, as her own home is in shambles after the major quake. She goes there daily to straighten things out.

Each morning and evening we watch the news. Our daily lives are nose-to-nose with the immediate world around us, so seeing a larger picture is important. But even so, we are much more focused on day-to-day living.

As I said, in the morning Izumi usually heads to her home, while I set out to find food. Lack of rice is a big problem. But vegetables and protein are also high on the list. I know of a small four-generation grocery store tucked way back in a neighborhood with narrow, twisting alleyways. The chain stores on main streets are closed or only open a few hours each day due to lack of supplies. But smaller ones off the beaten track are more promising.

To my utter amazement and delight, this place was to open at 3 pm. So, I joined the line of people waiting for that hope-filled hour. The wind was fiercely cold and the wait almost two hours before I was able to enter the shop.

Very wisely, the owners were allowing only five people in at one time. They had food because of farmer relatives who had brought in a large truck of vegetables and fruit earlier in the day. Most places permit people to buy only five or ten items, but in this beautiful place, the owners, deep with understanding, did not set a limit.

It was a real delight to watch people come out of the shop with bags full of such items as potatoes, cabbage, daikon, carrots, yams, and other sturdy vegetables. The look of joy on their faces was palpable. I got my share, too, and as I pedaled home on my bicycle, I found another wee shop selling two-kilo bags of rice. So it was indeed a fortunate day. When I got back to Izumi's mom's home, we all laughed and clapped for joy.

Since I will have to move from this shack of mine, I wandered over to a real estate office nearby to let them know my desires. Miraculously it was open. The woman was there to clean up and also because there was running water. There was none in her home and with her daughter's newborn child, washing diapers was a problem. So she scrubbed nappies while we discussed housing for me.

To shift focus off my immediate experiences, please let me continue sharing beautiful, life-affirming things that are happening all around. I am ceaselessly in awe of the emergency infrastructure here. There are not enough supplies, which everyone knows, but the excellently organized system is running like clockwork to the best of its overstretched abilities.

To give a few examples, evacuation shelters are all over every city. Food, water, and heat are there, although very limited. Mats and blankets, again in short supply, are also there. People are collecting wood from damaged buildings and making fires for heating and cooking. Volunteers welcome evacuees and help in whatever way they can. Firefighters and policemen carry the old and injured into shelters on their backs. And shelters have designated leaders to head meetings and make decisions.

People in the shelters are supporting one another. They massage each other's legs and shoulders, sit in close circles for human contact, read stories to kids, or simply hold hands. They are grateful for whatever goodness comes their way. "I feel so fortunate. We are able to eat at least once a day," one woman said.

And people are being very creative. Some are out collecting snow in plastic bags. The water from it can be used to flush toilets or wash dishes.

Today one young able man, who was helping his parents clean up the remains of their home, was called into the reserves. He had no choice, but was not happy about this turn of events. But his mother said, "We need him here, of course, but his service to others, to many, is more important than for only us."

During the day people go out to search for missing family members. TV crews are there, of course, and often stop people for interviews. Emotional wounds are deep and vast. People's intense efforts to contain grief is painful to witness. No overt wailing. But tears and silence everywhere.

"Shigata ga nai" is a Japanese expression that roughly translated means, "It cannot be helped." It also implies a sense of enduring what is happening and of making the best of whatever situation you are in. That concept is an integral part of everyday life here, not only now, but always. This emergency situation is surely one of "shigata ga nai". And everywhere people are saying, "We have to soldier on. There is no other way."

Gambarimashou (Let's soldier on together)

with Love,

Anne

LETTER FOUR

March 18, 2011 (late)

Dear Family and Friends,

This letter is different from others I have been sending recently. It is more about me than about the remarkable Japanese people. Please forgive this side tracking and indulgence.

Yesterday I was given the chance to leave Sendai via buses arranged by the U.S. Government for American citizens. I was told about this option well past midnight and the bus was to leave across town from where I was at around 9 a.m. If I went, I would be allowed one bag. I would be taken by bus to Narita Airport, where literally thousands of frantic foreigners were struggling to leave the country. From there I would be sent to a nearby Asian country and then left to fend for myself. I would be charged for the bus fare from Sendai to Narita later.

Several family members and almost all of my foreign friends strongly urged me to accept this option. "The chance may not come again." "The situation is very, very critical." "You should leave." "You will be helping the country if you leave." "You can always stay with me." "You can always go back when this is over."

I used to be really good at making clear decisions, but with age I find that I seem to take in others' opinions more. Maybe, too, that comes from Japan's consensus building culture. So, with so many people urging me to go, go, go, I was up half the night suffering excruciating existential agony.

After eating breakfast, I raced over to my wobbly shack to call a very close American friend in the USA to talk and process this. I also wanted to check e-mails once more. En route a deep calm came over me and I sensed I was not going to leave. My American friend agreed entirely. He had been through war and knew what mass hysteria involved. "Wait until this madness is over. Then make a calm decision," he advised. "The situation seems black or white now, but maybe it is not."

Talking to him, I realized I was not going to jump into the tidal wave of fear and panic that was literally sweeping the entire world. I did not want to add to that kind of energy. Whether I was right or wrong, lived or died, I knew that I wanted to be part of something that was more constructive towards life itself and the world as a whole.

I also sensed that for me personally to leave would be like a person suffering from emotional, psychological agony and trying to run away from it. I have found from personal experience that that does not work. For me I have to wrestle with and within excruciating emotional experiences, not necessarily to "get through them" because maybe we never really do, but rather to be able to consciously incorporate them into who we are.

We are physical beings, of course, but there are other dimensions of our humanity as well. And for me at this time I feel ready to work out of another level of my being.

By chance, to encourage me, among my e-mails there was one, lone voice that was entirely different from all the others. It was from my Dutch "brother", who is a doctor. This is what he said. "Apparently the situation is such that many foreigners are moving away from Tokyo to Osaka, or even home abroad. This, to me, is not good. I would think that one would stay and see where one could be of help."

Those open-hearted, humanitarian words rung a bell with me. I realized other people had left and would leave with their own legitimate reasons. And that is beautiful in its own way. But for me, considering how long I have been here, the number of Japanese friends I have, and my age, this situation is not about saving my own skin. There is something much more profound going on. For me it is on a very deep spiritual dimension. Now, it seems, is a time to step out of a desperate rush to save myself. It is a very humbling opportunity to practice what the Japanese have been teaching me through their day-to-day behavior ever since I arrived on these shores. We are all important. We must think of ourselves as a group first and then as individuals in it. It is crucial to put others before oneself.

If I am able to truly live that perspective in this horrendous situation, and if one small layer of my enormous ego can peel away through this experience, then that, I feel, will be my way of serving others who are suffering in this unspeakably tragic time of our lives.

Love and Light,

Anne

LETTER FIVE

March 19, 2011

Dear Family and Friends,

Another day has passed Sendai. It was sunny and the wind was strong. It was also warmer. So people's spirits were better. We are learning from direct experience how many gifts we have given to us constantly: sunshine, air, water. And now in many places electricity, although gas for cooking will take about another month, or so they say. We have heard that some gas stations are open for a few hours a day. The lines waiting to get a few liters begin at 8 p.m. The stations open at 10 a.m. the following day. But now there is a bit of gasoline available. And that is so very hopeful.

Today a former student came over to my shack to help me pack up. I do not know when I will move, but I do know it is a must. So, the sooner things get prepared, the better. We chatted and laughed as we worked. She told me at her office people arrive at 9 a.m. and en masse set out to look for food. The lines and wait are very long, so the earlier you start, the better. After they get whatever food they can, they go back to the office and enjoy a happy lunchtime together. It is excellent for bonding. And she told me how refreshing it was that the usual Japanese formality is not in operation now. Things flow easily between everyone, no matter what rank they hold in this highly structured society. "This is so good," said my friend. "We are relating as human being first and foremost. Giving up our social hierarchy is really, really wonderful."

My friend Izumi and I also laughed last night about our bathing and clothing situation. We have been wearing the same clothes round the clock for about a week now. "Isn't it nice not to have to spend time thinking about what clothes to wear and what make-up to put on? And think of all the time we are saving by not taking baths," she said with an enormous grin.

Yesterday, Friday the 18th, marked one week since this disastrous situation began. At exactly 2:43 pm the entire country bowed their heads in silent prayer. This day will surely be a day of mourning and of deep reflection for years to come.

Every night notes sent by people looking for loved ones are read aloud on TV news. "Susuki Kiyoko of Kesen-numa, age 45, please go to shelter #4 if you can. We are waiting for you. We miss you and worry about you."

After that the names, ages, and place of residence of the dead found that day are read. There are hundreds or thousands, so the reading goes on for a long time. It is very important, not only so people can know who have died, but also to give a sense of honoring those who have lost their lives in this very tragic time in Japanese history.

Slowly people are coming round to accept what has happened. And many of them are saying, "OK. This is how it is. How can we start to build our lives from here?" In one evacuation shelter high school students who still have homes come to volunteer their services. Many sports teams are donating all the income they receive from games to reconstruction work. And one soccer team donated their shirts, all personally signed, to shelters. They were a real pick-up and point of pride for those lucky enough to get one. True to the best of Japanese spirit, there was no sign of jealousy towards those with these bright, signed shirts. Rather people commented on how nice they looked or how useful they might be. Also ski areas have donated their rental skiwear, such as jackets, warm trousers, socks, and boots.

One older man who lost everything goes around, not only in the shelter, but also in what remains of his village to greet everyone he meets with a bright smile and a chat. He encourages all those he talks to. When interviewed, he said, "If I did not do this, the grief would cave in on me and possibly crush me. I cannot and will not let that happen. I hope that by helping others I, too, will survive this and build up a positive attitude."

As I mentioned before, the government is encouraging people to get back to as normal a life as possible. So, companies are open to the extent that they can be, even if that is only a few hours a day. Or as in the case of my former student, that might mean searching together to find food and to be supported emotionally.

I went to the post office the other day to get boxes for moving. There were about ten employees there and only I as a customer. But they were all dressed in uniform and as efficient as always. But since they had so much time on their hands, two of them offered to carry my newly bought boxes home. As a surprise treat we managed to buy some vegetables in a small shop en route. We all were delighted, of course.

Likewise, postmen are delivering mail whenever they can. There is not much, but they do try to keep the system moving. They are now using bicycles or walking because there is no gasoline for motorbikes and cars, which they usually use. In one place most of the houses had been damaged, but if a mailbox was standing, the postman delivered the mail, which was mostly advertisements printed up before the earthquake stuck.

People are siphoning off kerosene from wrecked boats, if they can, and using it for heating. Wood from the debris all around is also used.

Police and firemen wander all day through the piles of ruined towns and cities, looking for bodies, hoping to hear a voice. Last night they uncovered a 20-year-old man, who had managed to stay alive for so many days. Such small miracles make everyone feel that somewhere, somehow there is hope.

In fact, one man went back to the site of his factory, which was nothing but rubble. He looked around and said, "Here is where I will build the front door. And over here I will have my workspace. In the back I will set up the factory. But this time I will arrange it in a more efficient manner." He is truly a man living with concrete dreams. And I hope he will be able to make them come true: for himself and as an example for thousands of others like him.

Love,

Anne

Letter Six

March 20, 2011

Dear Family and Friends,

Last night the moon was full and very bright. Temple bells echoed through this city at 9 p.m. sharp, just as they always do. Today is the Spring Equinox. For Japanese people the Spring and Autumn Equinox are times when the divide between "the other side" and here is a bit thinner. So, ancestors' spirits come very close to earth to bless the living and to be blessed by them. This year is a particularly poignant time for such a crossover between worlds because of so many who have recently lost their physical lives.

This morning early Izumi's uncle came over asking for incense. He wanted to pray at the family altar, where Izumi's father's picture is placed to watch over the household at all times. Later he would go to the family gravesite to honor all those who had come before him. We will do the same, but in our own way. Today we are too preoccupied with attending to matters urgent to life here on earth in the immediate present: searching for food, sorting through the mess still all over our homes, and I packing to move.

Japanese vision extends back so far that it is able to take this moment in time and put it into a much larger context. Yes, the problems now are horrendous and ongoing, but they are not the end. Everywhere, there are signs of hope, of reconstruction, and of close, loving care. Thousands have died or are missing, but somehow life goes on.

When this all began, Izumi kept telling me that she remembered stories of her parents and relatives about World War II. "They lived for years on so little. At times they ate one rice ball a day. There was constant hunger and fear. But they survived. And we have Hiroshima and Nagasaki. They are perfect examples that things do not stay bad. They come back to life and things go on normally. Bad things are happening now, but we will survive and things will get better again."

Spring itself is a time of life's renewal. And in Japan the school year ends in late March, while a new one begins in early April. Even though many families and homes have been lost or damaged beyond repair, many schools are holding graduation ceremonies. Most are humble affairs, with students sitting on the floor and the principle handing out certificates from a makeshift podium. But the ceremonies are taking place and the students are being honored, as they should be.

On one such occasion a high school in Sendai gathered together its choral group, which sang before parents and other students. The songs were about the strength of Japan and how her spirit will continue through all of us. They were about hope and venturing out into the joys and challenges of life with courage and a positive spirit. There were also verses about cherry blossoms and the ethereal beauty of Spring and the promise of new life. The students and parents looked exhausted, many wept, but there was a timeless beauty of the enduring spirit of humanity on every face there.

Besides news of the developments of the nuclear power plant meltdown, TV shows now focus on stories of individuals. Some show families still seeking for lost ones. Others are about returning to where homes and work places once stood. Some are about family members reuniting after believing all had died.

There are other stories, too. Army tents have been set up with bathing facilities inside. Those in evacuation centers can go there for a good soak and a much needed time to relax. The smiles and sighs of relief are palpable on the faces of those privileged to have the sacred pleasure of a warm bath.

One group of people found themselves stranded with no way to get to a shelter. So, they banded together and made their own community. They collected wood from broken houses to make fires. They rummaged through rubble to find packets of food. And since one member was a hairdresser, who miraculously found her scissors, everyone was able to get a nice trim haircut. Simple pleasures, immense joys.

Again, normalcy is what people are striving for, even if in form only. Astonishingly, each day a newspaper arrives. It is thin, but crucial. There are photos and articles on how things are progressing, information on where food can be found, on medical centers, on places where people can bathe.

Since there is no gasoline, or very little, people resort to bicycles or walking. Today as I was sorting through yet more things in my shack, I heard someone calling outside. I went to see who it was and was utterly astonished to see a new friend there, bringing food, and checking to be sure I was all right. I have known this person for less than a month, but he was concerned about me because I am a foreigner and living alone.

Today I was able to look at Internet news about things other than what is going on in Japan. I had not been able to do so before. I heard how tenuous things are in the Middle East, even more so than before. And I felt sickened. This situation in Japan is very, very difficult, pulling most of us down to the very core of our being. It is peeling away any excess and bringing us to our knees, where we are forced to live from a place of complete honesty. Yet war is far worse. Here in Japan we have a sense of trust. We have each other. We are all working as a unit to get through this. And we will all work together to build a better future. We have hope.

As I continue to pray and work for Japan, I also pray that the world will wake up. All of us. During this time of great intensity and focus, the Japanese are manifesting the best that humanity can be. Surely the rest of us can do the same.

Love,

Anne

LETTER SEVEN · TOKYO

March 21, 2011

Dear Family and Friends,

First I would like to thank all of your for your kind e-mails to me. I appreciate them very much. It gives me a lot of energy and courage knowing there is so much love and support. I would also like to thank all of you who want to send me things, such as food or batteries, warm clothes or blankets. I myself am fine. I have only lost my home. Everything in it is intact. I have everything I need, thanks to Izumi and her wonderful family. We are eating less than normal, but we are eating twice a day, sometimes more. So, please do not worry about me.

If you want to help, please consider donating to the Japanese Red Cross. They are doing an outstanding job, stretched to the limit, but soldiering on. The same can be said of the army, the police, firefighters, volunteer doctors from all over the country and abroad, and of course, average citizens. This intense focus on a single purpose is getting things done. Slowly, but things are moving forward day-by-day.

Several people have asked if they can donate to smaller, more local groups than the Japanese Red Cross. As of now I do not have specifics on that. But when I find out, I will let you know.

Many people seem to think all of Japan has shut down, been severely damaged, and is in dire need. Such is not the case. This problem is mainly in the Northeastern Region, Tohoku, of the main island of Japan, Honshu, on the Pacific Ocean side. Other parts of Japan are feeling some effects, of course. Since the nuclear center in Fukushima provided one-third of Tokyo's electricity, that city is now facing cyclical blackouts. People are a bit panicked there, so are stocking up on food. But essentially there is enough. The ports are open, and gasoline is available, as are water, electricity (at certain times) and gas for heating and cooking.

To reassure you, here is a message from a woman in Tokyo:

"I have nothing to complain about. Compared to the tsunami/ earthquake-hit areas, this is heaven. We have everything we need, and even with the "threat" of planned power outage, we haven't once lost power. The morning papers are delivered right on time every morning. The Co-op my mother belongs delivers food orders delivered every week. Gas stations I believe are closed, but buses and trains are running, so we can go to stores or to visit my mom in the hospital. Rice, emergency food supplies, batteries, flash lights, portable gas stoves, and all those things are still missing from stores, but there is plenty of other food to eat. The weather has been really sunny, which is good for the mood.

"I just find it emotionally stressful, knowing all the suffering, pressure from my Canadian family to get out of here, but my Japanese family being so happy that we are actually here, trying to 'run' my parent's household, cook 3 meals a day, and still squeeze some time to work!

"Yesterday, we were in Machida, which is a rather big shopping area, and there were students all over near the station asking for donations for the victims of the earthquake. If I didn't know better, it was like a school competition, and they were having fun, and people were really giving. Almost all the prefectures are using their empty public housing to accept as many families as they can as far as Okinawa.

"TV stations are reporting news other than earthquake, and starting to show normal programming. I hear supplies are starting to reach the shelters. Japan Railway has devised a route going north on Japan seaside instead of the usual routing, Coast guard has used a hover craft to reach from the ocean, hundreds and thousands of trucks are on the way.

"We are just holding our breath for the good news about the reactor...

"I really hope something good will come out this devastation."

And in a subsequent message she added:

"I think what I tried to say was that for the first time in a long time, I am feeling hope for this country and younger generation. It's a strange time to be feeling that, but I see all these young people volunteering to collect donations, trying to help others. I think that will, and I hope, revitalize this country.

"They are doing all they can to put the nuclear reactors under control. Tokyo Fire Department has sent 100 extra fighters, so has Osaka Fire Department. Some power is restored to the reactors, and 2 of the 6 reactors are now under control."

. . .

Knowing other areas of the country are functioning normally is encouraging. It is an important reminder that we, too, will someday "get back to normal".

Love,

Anne

LETTER EIGHT · DONATIONS – LOCAL & OTHER

By their very nature, disaster relief efforts and how aid is best delivered to those most urgently in need are always and invariably rapidly evolving processes. Thus much of the disaster relief information that Anne originally suggested in this letter has since been superceded. Instead, we wish to thank you or whoever purchased this book – and to offer our assurance that the ongoing efforts it funds were specifically chosen for their effectiveness in getting various forms of aid to those who truly need it most.

However, we felt strongly that the efforts of one, particular individual and the organization that he founded many years ago should be presented as they originally appeared herein. Please also see Letter Twenty-Five for more about Imai Seiji Sensei and Yomawari, the organization he founded – and their extraordinary, humanitarian efforts, primarily on behalf of the homeless population of Sendai, Japan.

. . .

March 22, 2011 (early)

Dear Family and Friends,

Many of you have been asking how you can help the Japanese in this time of great trauma. Some have contributed to the Japanese Red Cross or to Doctors Without Borders. However, others write and said they would prefer to give to more local groups, hoping that most of the funds would go directly to the people with the greatest need.

If you would like to give more locally, here is one avenue that you can follow.

www.yomawari.net. This organization was started by my dear friend, Imai Seiji Sensei. I wrote about him in one of my first, online articles for odemagazine.com (now odewire.com). In fact, he was the very first person I presented in my blog posts. Imai Sensei started a homeless center here in Sendai several years ago and now includes victims from this disaster in his humanitarian work. This organization is very honest and transparent, and almost all funds are used for those in need. There is very little overhead in this NGO, which is staffed mostly by volunteers. This site will be in Japanese, but if you look on the right, you will see "Donation + Article" where you can find full details on how and where to send money or much needed goods. Also if you scroll down on his site, you can see local photos of this disaster.

. . .

Another friend also added:

"I must say it is very difficult for any group or prefecture to accept things from individuals at the moment.

It needs lots of man power to sort out accepted things, besides petrol is so hard to obtain now and there is no method to send things to each city or town which is damaged.

The best way to support people who have been suffering is to donate MONEY, not things."

. . .

Thank you all for your ongoing concern and efforts for the victims of this tragedy. Your love and contributions will improve this situation more quickly, I am sure.

Love,

Anne

LETTER NINE

March 22, 2011 (late)

Dear Family and Friends,

This morning on TV we watched a baby being born. The mother was an evacuee in a shelter, but miraculously had been able to get to a hospital when labor began. It was so joyous to watch this teeny girl emerging into the world and to hear her first loud, healthy wail. The camera shifted from the infant to the smiling face of the nurse and on the rather stunned, but pleased expression of the father. Life goes on. And everywhere there are efforts to remind us of that reality, even in these times of great disaster and tragedy.

Signs of hope continue to flood in from all sides. Yesterday an 80 year-old woman and her 16 year-old grandson were dug out of the rubble of their home, nine days after the tsunami hit. They had been trapped in their kitchen, so were able to survive on the bit of food they could squeeze out of their refrigerator.

In Kesennuma all the surviving fishermen got together and started planning how to reorganize their livelihood from the sea. They joined with the sellers of the early morning wholesale market. And as a group they began laying the foundation for a new system for the fishing industry in their area.

TV news is very informative with maps, diagrams, scale models of the nuclear site and devastated areas. Experts answer questions and give clear, simple-to-understand explanations. And they make sure to have stories about the survivors and their courageous attitudes and actions for survival.

People in evacuation centers are interviewed each evening. All of them express their gratitude and thanks to those who rescued and are caring for them. Many ask for family members to contact them if they can. And all say that life in the shelters is slowly improving. In one a beautician has figured out a way to wash people's hair, for example. And in another volunteers put on clown shows to give everyone a good laugh. In some centers everyone is sent elsewhere for a few days so the place can be cleaned and repaired. Much of that work is being done by high school volunteers. Likewise, the army and Red Cross have brought in hundreds of portable toilets, which are very needed.

Last night, too, tankers filled with gasoline arrived in Shiogama, a port just south of Sendai. Once gasoline is available to the average citizen, things will change considerably. But first it will be used for emergency vehicles, of course.

The government has sorted out alternative land routes to get to this area. The main road up the backbone of Honshu Island is in disarray, and the branch roads off of it to the Pacific coast are almost totally gone. So, now people make a huge loop around the western side of the island, going from Tokyo to Niigata on the Japan Sea. Then they swing either up the coast or inland towards Fukushima, Miyagi, and Iwate, the prefectures most strongly hit by the earthquake and tsunami. Transport must go by small, circuitous back roads. But eventually they arrive. Many people are coming up from Tokyo, bringing huge bundles of food, clothing, blankets, and medical supplies for their families. The trip, which in normal circumstances takes about five hours, can take longer than thirteen. But those few extra hours seem irrelevant considering the enormity of need.

It was encouraging to hear that young people have stopped carrying make-up and cheesy photos of each other in their handbags, but rather have water, flashlights, extra batteries, and high-energy snacks. They are devoting their time to helping their families and others in need. "This is a time I must support my family," they say. "I need to be there for them."

Before this catastrophe I knew that Japan was a culture of the collective. But I had not deeply comprehended what that meant. I used to accept, but wonder about students having club activities that took up almost all of their free time, including before and after school, weekends and holidays, and even cutting into study time. But when I see them now, able to work together in obedient unity, I can see how everything in this culture fits together. Somehow having students appear in uniform, all working together, seems to give a sense of stability. It is like strong steel pillars holding up a house. Civil servants are also all wearing blue or beige workmen uniforms. At this time of crisis everyone is equal; everyone is doing their level best to hold this country together and to move it forward.

There are still enormous problems. Children looking for parents, people living in cars or trucks, not enough food or medicines, thousands still unaccounted for, tens of thousands in shelters. Rows and rows of dead waiting to be blessed and buried. But the careful, panic-free, step-by-step work towards recovery is happening and will continue to do so, I am sure, for many, many more years to come.

Love,

Anne

LETTER TEN

March 23, 2011

Dear Family and Friends,

All of the letters I have sent so far have been my own. Recently I received the following e-mail from a former student, who is now an adult and friend. She give things from a Japanese perspective, so I would like to share her words with you. She gave me permission to do this and told me she was grateful if she might be able to help foreigners understand the Japanese mind a bit better.

Here are two letters exactly as she wrote them to me:

"Dear Anne,

I am sorry that I haven't been able to write back to you.

Sometimes I do not feel good enough to check e-mails. Sometimes I do not have energy to do.

Today I feel a bit better.

I realized that I get tired easily. Maybe I have to eat a bit more.

My emotional waves go up and down. But I am okay. I am dealing with it day by day.

Anne, I really appreciate you that you are sharing your letters with me also.

Your words are helping and encouraging me.

More importantly, it gives me bigger picture in some ways. Your words are helping my brain to comprehend this event better.

I heard that in the center of the Sendai city, shops are opening more and more.

Thank you for sending me the translator needed ad. Actually I was wondering about it.

I mean, when I saw the news on TV that Japan started accepting rescuers and volunteers from overseas,

I thought "how can they communicate? Maybe English/ Japanese speakers are needed??"

Half of me is wanting to apply. But unfortunately or fortunately, I am going to work from tomorrow.

Yes, I am going to work from tomorrow.

Maybe it is better for me to go to work instead of staying here all day.

My co-worker told me that there in no Internet yet at work so that mostly cleaning, organizing offices/desks. So I hope that it is not too much for me.

I used my microwave to make hot water. I put them in a big pot! I did it yesterday to wash my hair. Today for wash/wipe my body. I guess I am somewhat decent to go to work now. (grin)

Anne, I was so happy to read your letter and know that you decided to stay here.

I saw the news on TV that many foreigners are leaving/left around this area... some go south, some go out of Japan. now I know some of my foreign friends did it for temporarily.

I know their home country is warning them and advising them to do so. Nothing wrong about it.

HOWEVER, when I know the fact for the first time, I was deeply sad, almost shocked... and also I was in panic... and tears came out of my eyes.

I cannot know exactly what triggered me to have such a emotional state, but I did.

At the same time, Japan is getting so many support and donations from all over the world.

People do care about us. That brings very warm feeling in me.

Furthermore, Japanese people are uniteing more and more. I never ever imagined it.

I am proud of Japan and Japanese."

. . .

And here is a letter she sent the following day:

"I am at work. I feel satisfied to just come to work today.

Actually, I am just kinda sitting here, "not" working… but I feel better.

During my lunch break, I walked around. I was so surprised. I see more foods and supplies!

My co-worker and I went to Asaichi (near the Sendai station) to get some fresh vegetables.

Wow, so many vegetables with relatively fair price! I can shop like as usual! At the Asaichi, I saw fresh fishes as well. That was jaw-dropping!

Then, I headed to Yodobashi. I got an electric cook stove! and some light bulbs. Then, I got body soap, toothbrush, hand soap at one of the drugstores around there.

I felt much much better. wow... Now I know where to go to get some stuffs. (Around my apartment, most of the stores are closed or need to be in line so many hours to buy. So today's findings are amazing!)"

...

With Love from my dear student/friend and from me,

Anne

Letter Eleven

March 24, 2011

Dear Family and Friends,

Today was very bright and sunny. The winds were high, which somehow made it be a perfect March day. It snowed a bit, too, adding to the dramatic flavor of this new season. Also a few plum trees in sheltered areas were bravely shivering their pink blossoms, giving us promise of greater beauty ahead.

Yesterday was a rather nose-to-nose-with-this-reality sort of day. The water pipe to my shack finally gave way completely after days of slowly seeping water. My yard was a lake and then piles of mud as men, lucky to be found when other places are in much greater need, trampled through trying to stop the flood and repair the plumbing. They did just enough to keep me going until I find a place and can finally set up a new home. This shack has been my heart and haven for the past fifteen years. Hard to say good-bye, but it is indeed time to move on. Not only from here physically, but also to another dimension of my inner life. It is time for change on so many levels.

Coupled with that the wall holding up Izumi's home has been sliding more and more each day. Quakes have not stopped since this all began. And rain or snow comes off and on. Yesterday and this morning the rumbling was strong and frequent. So, Izumi was with workmen at her place all day, too. At night we swapped stories of how things went. For her, much more work ahead and expenses to be paid through the rest of this life, most probably. Poor Izumi, her situation and many others like it are yet another ongoing aftermath of this great and terrible natural disaster.

But fun things happened, too. A friend's husband went to the country and got eggs. He did not get enough for only his own family. Rather, he came back with 240 of these perfectly formed white oval gems. They were magnificent. He and his wife spent the evening going to the homes of family and friends distributing these rich sources of protein to those they loved. We all laughed out of sheer joy when they arrived at Izumi's home.

Yesterday, too, American helicopters began distributing boxes of supplies to shelters that are inaccessible by land. It was so touching to see huge American servicemen handing boxes to tiny little Japanese grandmothers and grandfathers. Neither could speak each other's language, but the old people held the hands of those giant creatures before them, bowed deeply, with tears in their eyes, saying, "Arigatou gozaimasu. Hontou ni kansha shite imasu." ("Thank you. We are deeply grateful to you"). Then everyone waved their good-byes as the men boarded the helicopters. Even the tough-looking Americans in their army fatigues seem moved and waved a fond farewell to those gentle people in such great need.

The same news reporter has been on TV every night since this whole thing began. We all joke how he seems to be aging rapidly. It looks as if he is about 30 years older than when he started reporting thirteen days ago. We are waiting for his hair to turn white and deeper wrinkles to form. But then we think of ourselves and realize we are not much different. Today I took a look at my fingers and was shocked (and amused) to notice how torn and rough they have become. "Shikata ga nai." (It can't be helped). So I smile and feel all the more part of this community of brave souls.

Whenever there is an earthquake, a loud beeping and red light flashing are broadcast on TV. This morning there were more strong ones in Ibaraki Prefecture and we felt them here a few seconds after they hit down there. It seems the center of the tremors is moving south, but we still feel the effects here a lot. We live alert, yet very grateful to be alive and OK every second of every day.

Izumi explained to me yesterday that one added problem is that Japan has two different electric currents. According to her, after WWII the USA set up one system on the east coast, while a European country set up a different one in the west. The Fukushima Nuclear Plant is on the east side and serves much of Tokyo. Now that that source of electricity is mostly down, it would make sense to get energy from elsewhere. But since the unaffected west coast is on a different current than Tokyo, it is not as easy as it might seem. The Japanese will figure something out, I am sure, but it will take time.

I remember once when a friend came to visit me here a few years ago. She was taken by how inwardly focused the Japanese tended to be. On public transport, for example, people usually sit quietly reading or playing with their cell phones. There is very little talking. That inward focus seems much more intense these days. People are caring for each other, yes, but the general attitude is one of turning inward and conserving energy for the long haul. I find that both practical and beautiful.

I also find it instructive how flexible the Japanese can be. They seem to be rigid when it comes to the structure of their social order with proper ways for doing everything. But as soon as a situation changes, these people are quick to adapt those seemingly hard-set rules to what is expedient at the moment. Japanese know that everything is relative to the situation at hand. And now it is for survival and getting back on our feet.

We will. I am sure of it.

Another lovely thing is a repeated advertisement on TV. The usual buy-this-buy-that sort of ad is completely inappropriate now, so the station has cut that type of bombardment out completely. Instead it plays an important message that goes like this: "Whatever lies in your heart can only be seen when it is expressed outwardly. Please be kind to others."

Love,

Anne

LETTER TWELVE

March 25, 2011

Dear Family and Friends,

Today marks two weeks since the great quake and tsunami. We still are shaking. In fact, just before I began this letter, I had to run out of my home because it rumbled and rattled too much for comfort. But even so, somehow it seems as if a shift has begun. Intensity is being replaced by resolution, along with the long hard work of both grieving and rebuilding our lives.

Since the highly concentrated stress of the past two weeks is slowly dissipating, these letters will probably become fewer as I, too, move into the next phase of my life: looking for a new home and then moving into it. Today I began that search. Old houses now, which have the most "kokoro" (heart, feeling) are too dangerous to live in now, and not worth repairing to make them safe. Rent on a new house would be much too expensive for me. So, do I consider an apartment? Would I be able to shift into that more restricted kind of mentality? Could my heart still sing if I lived in a box?

One problem after another seems to be coming Japan's way now. But just as the Japanese spend years learning how to write characters, sometimes having to distinguish one from another by only one teeny stroke, they are dealing with this situation using the same meticulous precision and attention to details. Learning how to write basics takes about six years, or more. And that is far from the end. Now, too the challenges being faced will demand the same sort of persistence and patience to achieve any sort of breakthrough. But

"Shikata ga nai" (There is no choice). We are where we are and we can only go forward from here.

Volunteer workers are going from one evacuation shelter to another on foot. They are trying to get statistics on who is where and what they need. But the populations in those centers keep shifting as people move daily and needs change just as quickly. "This task is unbelievably difficult," said one worker, "But we cannot and will not give up. People depend on us and we must help them."

Many shelters still have no water or electricity. Yet performers come to entertain the evacuees, students arrive to help prepare and hand out food, kids are given chocolate, and old people get massages. Exercise classes have started, led by yoga teachers. Kids draw and people write messages, which are posted on notice boards and read on TV.

In evacuation centers people at least have each other. Those in their own homes are often very isolated and grow depressed and desperate. So, establishing communication links as quickly as possible is imperative.

All over the country people are doing what they can. For example, a bicycle company has donated hundreds of bicycles, making sure they have very strong tires since punctures are a big problem with all the rubble on the ground.

The Tokyo government has given bottles of water to families with babies. Trucks with loud speakers cruise through the city telling people not to use tap water for infants, even for bathing. News constantly tells people not to panic, but to go about doing things with as much equilibrium as possible. "We must work together to solve our problems. You can only help if you stay calm and strong."

One very touching club was started in a shelter by a young boy living there. He asked the other kids if they would like to write a group diary. One child would write a message each day and read it to the group. When the school year ended, which is happening at this time in Japan, they would call that the end of stage one. Then they would bury the diary. And in ten years' time they will come back, dig up this treasured item, so full of poignant memories, and read it together. Then they could clearly see how far they had progressed in that measured length of time. Making those entries gives a tremendous sense of purpose and a vision of a future for these lovely souls who have lost so much.

People in badly damaged areas are still looking for family members, still living in shelters, still cold, still eating minimally. Yet in other places life is every so slowly, albeit unevenly, coming back together. There is more food available, and waiting lines are shorter. Shops, although not well stocked, are open a bit longer. And gasoline is gradually making its way to the average citizen, even though people still have to wait five hours or more to have a turn at the pump. (Lines start forming in the wee hours of the morning, or even the night before.) Soon gas will be turned on again, which means cooking and bathing will be more easily available.

Just as the human body needs its healthy parts to keep it strong and to promote healing, the Japanese government is spending much time getting the day-to-day infrastructure back in working order. Once that starts running again, their focus can be devoted more exclusively to the disaster victims, who are in such dire need. Now their efforts are in all directions. But soon, hopefully, they will be able to more fully concentrate on the earthquake-tsunami-caused homeless.

The nuclear disaster is another entire dimension of this tragedy. Its aftermath is reverberating all over the world and will not end soon. So many tough questions. So many avenues yet to open for alternatives.

In my own life, though, touches of beauty never cease. A friend, a man who gives massages, will come this weekend to ease Izumi's mom's aching joints. Despite the gasoline shortages, Izumi's husband, who works in his hometown, came back from his family home in the country for only one night to bring vegetables and water, an electric rod for heating water and news of places outside this city. Every night Izumi and I put down blankets and futons in neat rows, and then fold them up the next day. Working together like that, often silently, but always in perfect synchronicity, is very soothing for both of us. We call ourselves sisters and after this experience of my "being an evacuee" in her home, as she calls me, I can feel our connection more deeply than ever. The Japanese constantly live with a heart of "kansha" (gratitude), and thanks to this challenging time, I can feel myself moving more and more into that dimension, which rises up from the depths of my entire being. "I am because you are" has never been more poignant in my awareness.

A friend sent me the following poem, which seems so important to embrace at this time.

She said, "Here's a poem by an old Japanese poet, やなせたかし (Yanase Takashi). He's written many simple and lovely poems for children's songs. It was printed in the local newspaper."

Next to Despair Lies Hope! *(Zetsubō no tonari wa kibō desu!)*
絶望の隣は希望です!
By Takashi Yanase (1919 -)

Someone came silently

    And sat so gently beside DESPAIR.

 DESPAIR asked him,

    "Who on earth are you?"

Then the stranger smiled and answered,

    "My name is HOPE!"

   ...

With Love, as always,

Anne

We have since learned that Yanase Takashi wrote this simple, yet lovely poem in September of 2011 in response to the events of March 11, 2011 — which resonate with children and adults alike. Now 93 years old, he is still working as one of Japan's most beloved illustrators, writers and proponents of the anime art form — having created the Anpanman series, by far Japan's most popular anime character with younger children.

LETTER THIRTEEN

March 27, 2011

Dear Family and Friends,

Yesterday I went with a former student to volunteer at Imai Sensei's program for the homeless and evacuees. It had snowed the night before, so it was cold and very windy. But everyone arrived at the park on time. We were there to serve food and hand out clothing. For the homeless this has been an ongoing haven for several years, but for the evacuees it is still something rather new.

Since this program has been going on for a while, the people involved were very organized. Homeless men had been congregating for hours before a small truck arrived filled with supplies. Each man had a special task assigned to him, so the process of unloading the truck, putting down big blue mats, sorting used and donated clothes, and preparing the food tables went surprisingly smoothly. In fact, it ran like clockwork.

That day hot bean curry over white rice was the menu. The grateful homeless men and evacuees, some of them children, lined up and patiently waited their turn to be served. There was no pushing or shoving, no yelling or rudeness. Rather, everyone waited in quiet humility for the warm, filling meal they were about to receive. Then they scattered to available places in the sun, protected from the wind, to enjoy their food. Many went back for seconds and thirds.

After that nourishing meal was over, everyone again lined up to receive donated cup noodles, packaged rice porridge, and "hokkairo", which are small heating packs that do wonders against the cold. Again people were very gracious and grateful.

One of my favorite graphic art pieces is one by Fritz Eichenberg called "Christ of the Breadline". It depicts a line of men, heads bent down, hands folded, shoulders stooping from the weight of endurance in the face of ongoing poverty. Yesterday I saw people exactly like that. Everyone had on shabby clothes, some had no front teeth, no one's hair had been washed or combed. Yet, for me there was something much more, much deeper. Every one of those souls lined up seemed to have an inner beauty that glowed out of and around them. They seemed shy, deeply humble, and grateful for a chance to be recognized as worthy human beings.

Later an old man went to sort through the donated clothing. He was next to me as he bent over, trying to find a sweater. I turned and looked at him, and was reminded of my own aged father. I wondered how I would feel if my parent were the one looking through a pile of old clothes in a park on a cold spring day. I was so touched by that old, slow-moving gentleman that I almost cried. But I didn't. Instead I helped him select a nice black turtleneck and then assisted him in getting it on. He bowed deeply, and then his son came and together they walked away.

I wish I could say I saw only beauty as I volunteered, but there were vultures there, too. Some were middle aged people, rather well dressed, who would rather get free food than stand in long lines waiting to be let into supermarkets. One such that I found particularly offensive was a young, newly married couple who were there with the sole purpose of snatching whatever they could. They headed right for the hot food, then went round and round collecting other handouts. They had so many things that they needed a huge box to carry them all. I was furious and when they sneaked round to where I was to get even more handouts, I shouted at them and told them to get out of there. The Japanese volunteers had contended with the middle-aged "thieves" by saying,

"Are you homeless? Are you in a shelter? If not, then please wait until everyone else has had their turn." But I find that when I am angry, my American directness comes roaring to the fore like a raging dragon, and that is exactly how I behaved that day towards the young couple who brought shame to so many Japanese there. Later I apologized to the other volunteers, but even now I feel indignation and disgust towards those two, who left gloating over all they had gotten for free. It saddens me all the more when I realize that the terrible tragedy all around seems to have completely missed them. They seemed to be as superficial and as selfish as if nothing had ever happened.

But I will not let small snags like that get in the way of a larger vision, which I wish to see and to hold in my heart forever. There are now many TV programs showing work being done in shelters. Many concerts are being held, not only for charity, but also for the evacuees themselves. Sendai Philharmonic Orchestra recently held a concert in a shelter. "The sickness people complain of now are mainly of the emotions," one doctor said, "and music will sooth their minds for a while." And along a similar vein, school children in some shelters are forming choruses and singing in the evenings. Everyone longs for those moments of beauty, anything to give them courage to face another day.

Work on cleaning up is getting underway. Many in shelters are going to their former work places and starting to scrape up thick, oily, black mud from the floors and shelves. Others are sorting through the remains of their homes and offices to see what can be salvaged and put to future use. One delighted man found his computer with all his company data on it still in tact. Another young man said that even though he had a chance to go to college, he could not leave the people of his town. He would stay there and help them clean up and pull themselves together from scratch.

"This is where I belong. This is the work I am meant to be doing," he said.

Impressively we watched one small factory owner return to his destroyed plant, gather all his employees and give them a long speech. First he told them he was grateful they were all alive. Then he thanked them for all their years of service. From there he told them he could not pay them because he had lost everything, but if they would help him, he would do his very best to get his company up and running again and then they would have jobs once more. The men were so beautifully Japanese. They all stood in rows before him, heads bowed, hands clasped. They listened in silence and respect, knowing their boss was trying to help them to the best of his ability. Later the boss, once a wealthy member of the town, went to the bank to humbly ask for a loan to start all over again.

Stories like these are appearing more and more. Of course, there is still much grieving, much shock, much uncertainty. But ever so slowly, too, people are starting to pick up the pieces and move forward. Even the Emperor, who by tradition stays detached from the people, sent huge boxes of food and one thousand special eggs that are normally eaten only by the Royal Family. People say that was a sign of how serious this situation is, which of course is true. But I like to think that it might also mean that the current Emperor is sensitive enough to allow the most rigid social barriers to give way to compassion and the most profound depths of his own human heart.

Love,

Anne

LETTER FOURTEEN

March 29, 2011

Dear Family and Friends,

My friend Izumi is a remarkable person. She naturally embodies values that I wish I could incorporate in my own attitude and being. Because of what she is and does, I find it a real privilege to be able to spend this personal "evacuation time" at her mother's home, where she also is staying. Her husband works in the neighboring prefecture, Yamagata, and because of the gasoline shortage, comes here on weekends only. This is an unsettling period for everyone, so her mother is glad not to be alone. Therefore, both of us taking up lodging at her home works out well for all of us.

Let me give a few examples of the kind of person Izumi is. First, of course, she insists that I can stay at her mother's for as long as I need. "I will clear out my old bedroom and you can stay there. It is about time I sorted through all that stuff anyway," she said with a laugh. Currently my borrowed space in the house is in a corner of the "tatami" room on the first floor. Tatami are thick reed mats. Traditional Japanese flooring consists of these mats, which are made according to a standard size. I roll up my futon during the day and keep my things in one paper and two plastic bags. For me I feel it is good discipline to create a personal universe in such a small space. At least for a while.

The neighbors are rather concerned over the wall falling behind Izumi's home. It was made of huge stones, and formed a seemingly solid cliff to support the house. But it crashed down in the initial earthquake and has become more and more unstable as we continue having quakes everyday, some of them very strong. One set of neighbors in particular calls and complains often. They are a retired couple with a jobless son. They sit home all day looking at the huge boulders in their yard, wondering if more will follow soon. The clean up and repair jobs are taking time because companies are so busy in other far more damaged areas at this time.

This particular neighbor called to say another part of the small wall on his property had begun to collapse, and he was sure it was because of the larger wall above it. Would Izumi please come to fix it? So she and I spent one morning mending his wall. Afterwards Izumi said, "You know, if that had been me, I would have put myself in the place of the people who had lost their major wall. And I would have fixed this small part myself as a way to show my concern for them."

Later she had to go to the City Hall to report about the damage and to ask for some advice. The official there told her that if we evacuated the house, it would set up an alarm that the wall was very unstable and we would get help faster. But again Izumi thought of the fussy neighbors. "If I were those neighbors and the folks in the house above moved out, it would give me an even greater feeling of insecurity. It would seem as if they were running away, as if they were afraid. I don't want to cause them any more worries than they are now feeling. So, no, we will not leave here."

The reason I have not yet found another place to live is because official inspectors must come and check every building and each individual apartment in this city before they can be approved for rental. Also many people from the devastated areas are flocking into Sendai, looking for housing (and later for work, of which there has been a chronic shortage for several years). I had my eye on one magnificent spacious old place, but the woman took it off the market because her family in Fukushima needed a place to stay.

And I continue looking, as I grow more deeply appreciative of Izumi and her mother's generosity with each passing day.

Interestingly last night I learned that since the huge Kobe Kansai Earthquake in 1995, the federal government set up mutual aid between prefectures. Each area has a "sister" prefecture to come to its assistance in times of need. So, our "sister" prefectures further south have started sending experts to help us here in Fukushima, Miyagi, and Iwate.

Also adults from Kobe, who know from personal experience what is needed in times like these, have been sending busloads of volunteers. Last night we saw college students going into shelters with buckets of warm water to wash people's feet and allow them a good foot soak. Even though they could not fully bathe, the evacuees' sighs of relief were palpable. Just having warm, washed feet was sheer heaven. Another group donated pillows, some with encouraging messages. "Ah, how wonderful. Now I can sleep again," said one evacuee. And in Sendai City Hall there is a lovely display of artwork done by school children from Kobe. There are paper cranes, of course, and many pictures. But for me the prize is all the handmade books full of messages and drawings, words of "gambatte" (the imperative of "gambarimashou" meaning, "Don't give up" or "Soldier on") and hope. Somehow that connection of understanding helps us feel not quite so desperate or lonely.

And now it is our turn to learn so much about what really matters. As one of my students wrote to me, "I'm great because I can eat every meal, I can sleep in my bed, I can take a bath! I've took it for granted that I spend ordinary daily life every day, but this thought was fault. We should be thankful for our good fortune."

There are so many displaced persons now. There are tens of thousands in evacuation centers. Some friends not in Japan ask why they are still there. They do not seem to realize the depth and severity of this problem. In the first place, there are very few homes left to go back to. The land is devastated. The towns are in complete disarray with debris all over the place. There is often only one small track cut through the rubble to allow relief vehicles through.

Likewise, some oldsters totally refuse to leave their homes that have seen several generations born and die there. Last night we watched men covered in strong white protective gear going into old farmhouses near the nuclear plant, talking to the old people still there, telling them they had come to take them to a shelter. But the old people said they would rather die in their own homes than be uprooted and go live in a crowded, impersonal place like a shelter.

Another huge problem is that many of the evacuees do not want to leave the area where their families have been for generations. "Our family graves are here. How can we leave our ancestors? What will they think of us? How will we get protection from them if we pick up and leave? How will they find us? Where will we be buried if we do not stay near our beloved deceased?"

The Japanese truly live knowing the continuity of life. This tragedy is horrendous and will take years of work to rectify. But even so, they know that this is one of many such disasters. Not the first, not the last. Yesterday on TV I watched scientists and researchers going to the coast where villages used to be. They were studying the way building had fallen. By carefully observing the angles and direction of floors, walls and debris, they were piecing together the puzzle of how this monstrously forceful tsunami had operated. "This will help us in the future to establish better building codes. The old rules worked fine in the past, but this tsunami went far beyond all others in its intensity. So now we must adjust ourselves to this new awareness."

And ordinary life continues, too. Yesterday next to Sendai Station, which has been closed since the earthquake, a woman was planting pansies as a sign of spring and new life. They were beautiful. And so very full of color and of joy.

Love,

Anne

LETTER FIFTEEN

March 31, 2011

Dear Family and Friends,

Last night we watched the Emperor and Empress visit an evacuation shelter. This way of expressing care is a first ever for the royal family. As I mentioned in a previous letter, by long tradition they live in a world apart from the rest of us. Their public appearances, and their existence itself, are symbolic of a Cosmic order that manifests in perfect precision and harmony. Happily this far-reaching tragedy is allowing them to open their hearts and to express their concern on a very human level.

In the shelter, the Emperor actually squatted down to be on the same level as the evacuees. He also looked at them directly as he spoke to them. His gracious wife stood, but bowed down very low in order to talk closely and warmly to the people there. She extended her hand and held those of others in hers. That sort of behavior is unprecedented here. And it was indeed very symbolic, but on an entirely different dimension than the usual meaning of the royal family's behavior. It brought so much hope and encouragement to everyone who experienced it in actuality and who watched in on TV.

There are other stories of amazement, too. My friend Izumi was very worried about one of her friends who had been missing since March 11. She and I had planned on going to find her as soon as the roads opened up. The other day Izumi was at work. Her job is to explain about the special scholarship that is being offered at her university to people who have lost their homes or jobs because of the tsunami. One call was transferred to her. To her utter astonishment it was her lost friend! Izumi's cry of relief could be heard a thousand miles. And then came the tears of profound joy that her friend was alive and well. She is now living in a shelter. But as she said, life must go on. In a shelter or not, she wanted her child to be able to attend school.

Another incident occurred that might make you think angels are hovering all around us at this time. The grandson of one of Izumi's friends was living in Kesennuma. When the tsunami hit, he ran for his life. And en route to higher ground, he fell and got badly cut, but he kept on fleeing with all his might. As he was running, he came upon two old people also trying to flee. Normally he was too arrogant to give much thought to old folks, but at that time of great emergency, he grabbed the man, who could barely walk, and put him on his back. He took the hand of the old woman and ran with her as fast as he could. All three managed to get to a shelter high enough that the tsunami did not reach them. He made sure the old couple was OK, and then he collapsed. The following day he wanted to find them and see how they were doing. But they were nowhere to be found. And even more mysterious, no one had even seen them the day before. The people in the shelter are all convinced that the two old people were spirits of "kami", the gods, who came to save the boy's life. In olden times such appearances were said to be quite common. But these days we have lost touch with that world. Yet maybe in times of great danger, the veil between worlds vanishes and heavenly assistance comes very directly to us, in whatever form we most need.

I was fascinated when Izumi's mother told me that the emergency program in full operation now has a very long history. She is almost 88, and about 75 years ago there was a huge flood in her part of town. Everyone raced to the temple, which was on the highest hill and served as an evacuation center in times of emergencies. Within hours people who had not been affected by the flood arrived and gave them water, rice balls and blankets.

Izumi explained that since the Edo Era this program has been in operation. At that time along with earthquakes and tsunami, there were huge problems with fires. Houses were all made of wood and stood very closely side-by-side. If a fire started in one, it would race through and burn down all the homes. So, the firemen would race to the scene and completely demolish a home as soon as it caught on fire. That way, hopefully, the flames would not get out of hand and destroy the entire village or neighborhood. That was when this system of care during emergencies was first set up. And since rice farming requires a community effort, everyone was willing to help others because everybody's survival depended on it.

And that mutual cooperation is happening everywhere now. The cohesive power of it is truly amazing to watch, sense, and directly experience. With over 800,000 either dead, lost, or in shelters, the aid being given is stretched to full capacity, but it is happening. And it hopefully will long after the intensity of this emergency is over. Healing is going to take a long time.

But one very beautiful change is that we are grateful for the small blessings that come to us naturally and unasked for. Sunshine today, more food in the markets, a place to sleep, the love of family and friends. People can be so good. And this time is allowing that inner beauty to shine forth everywhere. So many are now saying, "I am so blessed to be alive."

Love,

Anne

LETTER SIXTEEN

April 1, 2011

Dear Family and Friends,

Many people overseas keep asking me about the nuclear situation here. In these letters I have not been addressing that issue for several reasons. One is that the international press seems to be mainly focused on that problem, so people are surfeited with that news. Also the situation changes by the minute, so it is hard to keep pace with the latest developments. But more deeply, I have not dealt with that intensely emotional topic because my purpose in writing these letters is a bit different. I wish to show the beautiful dignity of the Japanese people through these traumatic times. For me this experience is on the level of the soul and of the heart. And despite the worldwide concern and fears over the nuclear spillage, I wish to consistently focus on the inner strength and courage that are being manifested all around me and that might not be presented in regular coverage.

For us here we have to keep on living. We have to eat. We have to try to reassemble our lives after tremendous upheaval and loss. As I wrote to one of the editors of Ode Magazine (now odewire.com):

"People are concerned about the radiation, of course, but here in Sendai we are trying to get our lives back together from scratch, many of us literally. Just getting food and water was a major concern until a few days ago. Even now supermarkets are mostly empty except for fresh vegetables, although they are open. People who live close to the nuclear plant are having to vacate and go live in shelters, with no limit as to when they will ever leave. We are nose to nose with daily living now. And the quakes go on and on and on, sometimes very strongly even now.

"The international press is going wild with the radiation news, but we here have to go on living all the same. And I should add that Sendai is being flooded with people from the devastated areas coming to find a place to live. It is in many parts like a city of refugees.

"Please try to understand where I am coming from, even though the international audience is mostly focused on radiation fears. We are, too, but it is only part of what we have to deal with now. We are still trying to locate family, friends, students, employees, not knowing if they are alive or not. Mass funerals and burials are happening everyday here. The energy here is very jagged."

And here is another message from my former student:

"Last week, I couldn't work at all. My mind and head was elsewhere. However, I am getting some work to do, etc. So I am pushing myself a bit. Gradually. Everyday. Still, cannot focus on one thing for long time but my working-business head is slowly coming back.

"I can tell you this; I start feeling better each day. Somewhat I am still in shock of all this. Sunday night, I saw the news about a ship captain who operates a ferry between Kesennuma and Ooshima. People are leaving/evacuating from Ooshima, but the captain is asking them to come back because the small island needs people for recovery and rebuilding. His last comment: 'My ship named Himawari (Sunflower). Himawari always looks up and faces toward the bright sky/sun. I would do the same.'

"Tears came down from my eyes. I know some people are still facing harder times, still in a shelters, etc. I have my own apartment,

I still have a job, I still have income, I am still alive. I can feel positive at least. I mean, we need happiness, we need to feel secure. At least I can smile a bit each day."

. . .

I think those words portray what I have been trying to express. Truly words spoken out of the depths of very tough experiences, but consistently from the heart.

Love,

Anne

Letter Seventeen

April 3, 2011

Dear Family and Friends,

"The world is one." It seems that is becoming more and more true these days. Everywhere. And during this time in Sendai, I see it very clearly on so many levels. First of all, everyone here, and all over the country in differing degrees, is still feeling very shaken by the events that are still evolving here day by day. Actually this uneasy feeling is happening worldwide, too, as people continue to hear news of the nuclear power plant's ongoing problems.

But there are other more subtle ways in which "one world" is being felt. This region of Japan has predominately farmers and fishermen. In order to make ends meet, many folks started small businesses. So this area had many small factories dotted across the landscape. In fact, many large companies in Tokyo used those enterprises to make parts for machinery or other necessary goods. It was convenient for everyone since the small towns had easy access to train lines or ports, making it efficient to get things to Tokyo without problems.

However, the tsunami came marching in and took all that away. Most of these small factories are now completely rubble. And that means larger companies which depended on them are without very needed parts for machines, cars, and other products.

Before the tsunami, small paper factories were in abundance up here. Yet, when textbook warehouses got flooded or completely damaged, there was no way to make paper in order to replace the unusable books. Likewise with food. There might be vegetables, fruits and fish for the market, but the factories that made the styrofoam trays to hold them are no longer in existence. Establishments making cartons were also completely demolished, so milk cannot be delivered. Also now there is very little gasoline, so just getting products distributed is a huge problem. Everyday we hear of another link that has been broken in this "one world" chain. And it seems that it is being felt not only here in the tsunami stricken area, but throughout Japan, and worldwide as well.

The people still in shelters, and there are tens of thousand of them, surely know what "one world" means as they share space with others day in and day out. Scenes of those places are of a patchwork of blankets covering the floors with people crouched in the particular small spot allotted to them. No privacy, except for what bowed heads and lowered eyes of the neighboring evacuees allow.

Today repairmen came to check out the falling down wall that is more or less holding up Izumi's mother's house. They explained that fixing it would be problematic because of the neighbors' houses so closely packed in below. They went on to say that maybe everyone would have to evacuate to a shelter, all of us in Izumi's mom's and also the neighbors. "One world." "We are all in this together."

But this "one world" theme is being seen in happier ways, too. We are constantly hearing slogans like, "You are not alone." "Japan is one team." "We will not give up." TV adds show people with very positive attitudes talking about helping others in need. On the street there are signs everywhere saying, "Gambatte Miyagi, Fukushima and Iwate!" or "Let's work hard together today to make a bright tomorrow for everyone."

Since we are all feeling ongoing stress, we all want to be part of the solution. And people are coming up with creative ways to do so. Hair salons are giving free shampoos to everyone. People set up chairs on the street and offer shoulder and neck massages gratis. Since we still do not have gas for cooking, many miniature food stalls have sprung up all over the city. In the farmers' market today when the fruit seller learned I had lost my home, he immediately gave me a free bunch of bananas. "You deserve something to give you a lift", he said.

There are many other ways people are trying hard to lighten the load others have to carry. Usually carp streamers, celebrating children, are flown in early May. But huge ones have started to appear these days fluttering in the breezes over homes and evacuation centers.

One man's factory was completely lost, but the owner of another, who was more fortunate, offered him space in his own. There he set up shop, although now a much smaller operation. "I am so grateful to this man. Thanks to him I could keep most of my employees. I worry about them. They need to work. They need to get back to something reassuring. I am glad I can do this for them."

Teachers are very concerned for their students. Normally the new school year begins on April 1. But since many schools have either been demolished or are filled with evacuees, this year classes will have to start later. Even so, teachers have gone back to where their schools once stood, and have gone through the rubble to find their students' book bags. They then ever so carefully and lovingly clean them, and then deliver them individually to each child. Likewise, principals give graduation ceremonies in students' homes, one at a time. "This ritual is very important for the children," one man explained. "It is a marker for them that they have finished one phase of their life successfully and are embarking on the future. I feel I must do this to honor them and what they have been through."

Famous pop stars and actors go to evacuation centers to give performances. It is so moving to see the audience clapping, singing along, smiling, and even laughing, although there are many tears, too. But we all cry so easily these days. It is part of this deeply significant experience we all are going through.

I watched a middle-aged couple picking through mounds of rubbish that was once their home. Painstakingly they searched, eventually finding a photo album here, a box of jewelry there, kids toys in one spot, loved cloths in another. All were covered in sticky, oily, heavy mud. Somehow their work reminded me of the weight of depression. Taking in the whole picture at once is too heavy, too dark, too overwhelming. So they were doing the only thing possible in that situation. They were looking for a teeny bit of hope here, a small amount of happiness there. And then step by ever so careful step, hopefully, they will slowly work through their despair and into something with a sense of potential and of possibility.

Yesterday afternoon I walked though the forest park behind my home. I passed a pond that had many long reeds at one end and that was filled with ducks and huge orange carp slowly circling below. Children usually love to go there to feed those inhabitants, but at that time there was no one. As I made my way across a small stone pathway, my eyes caught sight of a large white bird. It could have been an egret, but I wished it to be a crane. For the Japanese the crane carries much meaning. Stories about it stretch the length of this country's history. I stood transfixed, watching this motionless creature reflected perfectly in the water below. Time seemed to stop. But then he would poke his long beak into the tangle of reeds and mud and pull up a teeny fish, a bit of life-giving nourishment. His instinctive actions seemed to parallel those of thousands of people here doing exactly the same as he.

After these moments of suspended time, he ever so graciously spread his wings and started to work them up and down, up and down. It took effort, but he was finally able to lift his huge body upward and to glide very smoothly overhead. He was beautifully poised and skillful, perfectly shaped as he soared in the sky above. I watched him and understood why he is a symbol of the Japan I deeply love. In my heart of hearts, I know that somehow that image will become reality as we work to lift ourselves out of the sadness and seemingly hopelessness of our current situation and into something that it truly magnificent and life affirming for all.

Love,

Anne

LETTER EIGHTEEN

April 8, 2011

Dear Family and Friends,

The following letter was written before last night's strong earthquake. But even so, much of it still applies. Last night's quake was very forceful. We either dove under tables or braced ourselves in door frames until the major trembling had ceased. The shaking continued on much longer, and tremors are still with us, as are non-stop sirens of ambulances and police cars. Yet, this quake was within "normal limits" for a strong one. Plus it did not last long. And the tsunami afterwards was "manageable". Even so, it did cause more damage. Walls are falling a bit more predominately, cracks are a lot wider, houses sway more easily. After the major quake of March we were told to expect another forceful one within a month. And sure enough, just shy of four weeks, this one came along. The last of this cycle? I doubt it. But hopefully the next ones will not be as strong, will bring less havoc.

This recent shaking up, I am sure, will solidify us all the more. If that can be possible. Already we are a tight knit group of survivors, volunteers, and relief workers. I saw on TV last night an entire tent city of university students who had come from all over the country to help dig out places covered in mud. They brought their own camping tents and food. The work they were doing is daunting and messy, but the wonderful young folks are doing it with an attitude of selfless service to those in need. They, and thousands of others like them. "Daiji tahatsu tero" ("multiple simultaneous terror") – but somehow these extremes are bringing out the very best that people can be.

. . .

Dear Family and Friends,

This may be my last letter for a while. Things are shifting. News is more and more about people rebuilding their lives. There is so much courage here. One of my friend's family lost everything but their lives in this disaster. Yet, this is what she just wrote to me.

As with other letters, I'm including this exactly as it was sent to me:

"my family and i have began to step forward. my dad is so strong to get himself back from the depression. im so proud of him. watching him this close makes me want to support him as much as i can more than before. i dont think he is expecting something from me but I feel that i gotta just live my own life and have my own family eventuarely. i hope so too.

"well, im with my family now and im going to utsunomiya this thursday at the earliest to start job hunting.

"im not sure where my family is going to live and neither i am but i will keep you updated."

. . .

I still need to write, though. It holds me together, allows the tsunami of events to be packaged into bite-size pieces. I could not handle it otherwise.

This upheaval is so unsettling, rocking us to our core. It is hard to focus, hard to feel settled inside. This tremendous upheaval is allowing unbelievable openness. Fully responsive to the now. Shell shock in many ways, but enduring. Possibilities, potential. Starting all over again. Heart so wide and deep it could embrace the Cosmic and everything within it. What have we learned? What are we learning? What will we carry with us through this? No one knows yet. We are still very much in process.

This letter, unlike the others, will be more rambling, more a stream of conscious rendition of what and how I am living day by day.

So many people are saying, " I want to help you", "If I can help you, please let me know." That is a standard way of saying good-bye these days. Lovely, but somehow unless I really need it, I do not want that now. This time is much too deep, the wounds too profound, too open. This is a journey we are all going through, yes, but also each of us is also alone. We each have our own pain, our own wounds, our own ways of experiencing all this. For me I curl inward. I write for connection to my soul and to others. I appreciate the company of Izumi and her mother. But my heart is too wide open, too raw now to really go over except on very, very deep levels. For me this is not a time for superficially being nice.

Bicycles are everywhere now. We still don't have full access to gasoline. I like to see everyone out pumping up and down hills. Only the young downtown are getting back into ridiculous fashion of high heels and much too revealing mini-skirts. They look more out of place than ever. And terribly superficial, especially considering what we are still going through. But somewhere under all that I hope that they were touched by the recent events, hope that somehow their souls, too, took one small step towards greater awareness, their individual selves towards maturity.

The devastation, the ongoing sorrow, are like depression thrown outward. The darkest recesses of the psyche are out in the open for all to see now. For all to deal with.

A friend of mine has been visiting evacuation shelters to see her clients. I told her I wanted to volunteer in a shelter. But she advised me against it. "I don't recommend you to see them. It was really disaster and as you know, a lot of dead bodies are buried these places. I have felt very tired since I passed through the places."

A friend who is working in an NGO on the Thai-Burmese border wrote to me and said:

"I can't help but think that your e-mails reflect life here in Thailand for Burmese ethnic groups on a regular basis - lines of people collecting food rations, blankets, living in confined spaces. I guess it must be difficult for ppl in Japan because it is such a sudden shock in their lives and their standard of living has changed so quickly. Here, many of the 20,000 refugees in the camp (20,000 of the 140,000 people living in refugee camps along the Thai Burma border) have fled from forced labour, their houses being burnt down, confiscated land etc. Many lived in the jungle for years before making it to the camps in Thailand. There's a great poem called Jungle University that I must forward onto you. Unfortunately there is no education after year 10 in the camps. Mental health is a big issue however many services seem to focus more on relief than development. Shame to meet many people born in the refugee camps and know nothing of life beyond the boundaries of the camp."

. . .

Suffering is a human condition.

And I do not want to shun those very significant, intensely emotional places like the evacuation shelters here in Japan. They seem to be where the deepest ongoing sorrow is happening. If I could go to one of those shelters to volunteer, I feel I could better understand the profound "kokoro" (heart) that is so openly being expressed these days, uninhibited by social protocol. I feel that would allow me to have deeper compassion for my students. Teachers here carry a huge role, far beyond the classroom. By tradition they are pillars of society; they offer lifelong support; they help students establish an identity connected to a lineage. So for me offering my services in a shelter would be a widening of the heart in order to be more deeply connected to those I am to work with when schools open once again.

All this is very disturbing. Very challenging, but also a golden opportunity to look, to reassess, to become more awake, to choose values consciously, to live life more poised in perfect center.

Off and on images come back to me of how it was just after this happened. There were people walking and walking. All in one direction. But where were they going? To evacuation centers? Home after work? Walking. And the Silence, the deep inward turning, the resolution to do what had to be done, instinctively.

Now in this neighborhood there is an old woman who seems to have had her whole being so rattled by this that she is completely unhinged. She gets out and walks all day. Up and down the hills, clothes half falling off, a mad look in her eyes. Izumi says she was always odd, but this situation has thrown her off more than ever. Izumi said her son disappeared for about 30 years and came back when he was in his 50s, only after his mother's long search, with no word of where he had been. He has vanished again.

A former student-now-friend works at Yamaya, an import liquor shop. Usually she sits behind a computer all day making international orders, but now she is in work boots and factory suits washing every bit of merchandize in the warehouses and stores, all of which got so muddy and mucked up. The slow, hard process of recuperating. She said when she first started she had many dreams of dead spirits floating everywhere. She believes they are of the recent deceased. After two days of it, she bought a crystal bracelet to ward of that disturbing energy. She says she is more protected now, more able to handle the jagged, unsettled vibrations everywhere now.

On TV every night we see cool young people, singers perhaps or athletes, saying, "The road ahead is long and difficult. But I am going to work hard to get through this. We will do this together. I believe in Japan." Everywhere we are encouraged to focus on what we can do to help this situation, to rebuild our own futures, those of others, and that of the country as a whole.

Those images are so important. They stand in hope-filled, determined contrast to what is next to them: more and more reports of the domino effect of all this. People in Tokyo can't finish building their homes or offices because the plywood involved came from factories now gone. The same for food packaging. Yogurt, milk, natto and other products like them all need special government approved cartons, which no longer exist. Rolling blackouts are causing havoc in factories that need ongoing electricity to complete their products. Every night we hear of yet another link in this chain being broken.

The moving man came to my shack to talk about helping me get from here to my new abode. He took a quick look and then said my house was much too unstable for his company to help me. So here we go again. Wondered what would emerge from this little wrinkle! I am determined to handle this the way I have seen so many others handle their problems: one careful step at a time.

So, I called both Izumi and Yoko, another good friend. Her husband is strong and has a van. Maybe he could help me. Izumi thought of others, and called a delivery company to see if they would mind moving me. It is all about connections at this point.

Izumi reminded me that here in Japan each day has specific energy pouring through it. Some are very good luck days, while others are bad. Some are neutral. And there are many subtle nuances of each type. She explained that no one wants to move on days considered unlucky, so they are the cheapest. I don't mind the fortunate or unfortunate energy running through my moving day. I have so many "Oni" masks (symbolizing stronger than strong, invincible, undefeatable) that I feel I will be protected no matter what.

And to our joy a delivery company said they would take the job. Friends' husbands will come. We plan to make a long relay line and pass boxes down it to the waiting vans. Oh, my beloved friends. How could I survive without them?

And that idea of linking, leads me to two final stories. One came from a friend in Tokyo, who has been very eager to help me. He is the one who told me not to feel embarrassed asking friends for help at this precarious time. It is part of the Japanese culture to help others, he reminded me.

This is what he recently wrote:

"I am reading your report on the latest situation in Sendai and people, and am very impressed. On 15/Mar, I went to Bangkok for a short stay to meet my friend. The flight from Haneda was fully occupied by foreigners who were trying to evacuate from Japan as quickly as possible.

"In Bangkok, I saw lots of Thai people's campaign, students in particular, to support people in Tohoku area. They say, 'Japan supported us best whenever we were in problem, particularly at the time of Sumatra Tsunami, therefore, we wish to do something for them'.

"Anne san, one good news is that Postal cargo deliveries to Sendai has been reopened, although they said no guarantee when the cargo can be delivered. One cargo is maximum of 30Kg, so, I can send you something you or your friends need, not possible perishable products though. Please do not hesitate to let me know what I should send."

. . .

Oh, my generous friends. I am so humbled.

And here is yet one more example of foresight and generosity. There was an old man who lived near an elementary school. Everyday he watched the children drilling on what to do when an earthquake struck. He saw them go out in disciplined rows to the schoolyard and then make their way down a small street and up to higher ground. The entire procedure took about five or seven minutes.

This wise gentleman had known many earthquakes in his lifetime, so knew that even half a minute could be the difference between life and death. So, he thought and thought about how to make a faster escape route for the children. After some time he came upon the idea of a bridge that would go from the school, over the houses, directly to the top of the nearby hill.

He discussed this for many months with the town officials, who finally agreed to his plan. About a year later this thoughtful man passed through transition, but the bridge was still there as a reminder of his farsightedness. Sure enough the big quake and ensuing tsunami hit and all the students followed what had been drilled into them over the years in school. They went obediently out of the school, across the bridge to safety on higher ground. Not one child was killed or lost. And among those survivors was the old man's grandchild. She is now immensely proud of her grandfather and said, "I am pleased that he was able to save us. He thought about us even before there was an emergency. I hope someday I will be able to help others the way my grandfather helped my teachers, my friends, and me."

Love,

Anne

LETTER NINETEEN

April 11, 2011

Dear Family and Friends,

I thought my most recent letter would be one of the last. But I am finding that writing my impressions and feelings allows me to put small frames around the enormity of life now. A story here, an image there, a sign of hope and courage elsewhere. All those teeny pieces, when held together, allow a crucial sense of equilibrium. Things seemed to be getting settled more or less, but then the second major quake arrived a few days ago, stirring everything up once again. Part of me would like this to stop. Others feel the same. There are signs around town now saying, "We have had enough, please stop shaking, Mother Earth." Or "How much longer?" But those queries are next to ones saying, "Gambatte Sendai" ("We believe in you, Japan" or "Our combined inner strength will see us through this").

The quake and tsunami of March 11 caused untold destruction. But this second one brought out the inner damage that the first left lurking below the surface. Far more walls have tumbled down, roads are more uneven, and more broken windows have left shattered glass all over the streets. Blue mats are everywhere now. They seem to be this year's koi-no-bore, carp streamers, which normally appear about this time.

But there is a shift, too. At first the main concern was to get people to safety, then to provide a place to eat and sleep. A great deal of effort was spent trying to locate the missing, dead or alive. As one barber from Kobe said, "The first week everyone is worried about water and food. The second they all want a bath. By the third week they want to have their hair cut. That is why I am here. And I brought my friend, a hairdresser, to give the ladies a nice shampoo and cut, too. This is our way to serve the survivors and bring them some joy."

Slowly things are evolving in other ways, too. Shelters are being consolidated, making it easier to service the inhabitants in them. It also makes it better for communicating important information. This is crucial, especially now, because there are still ongoing quakes with possible tsunami to follow. Plus some places do not have electricity or water yet, even though a month has passed since the first disaster. By bringing several shelters together, these problems should be rectified. Some people have already been moved several times. But even so, they bravely accept what comes to them and try to remain positive and appreciative. "We have food and a place to sleep. Things will get better soon, I am sure," said one determined woman.

Temporary homes are being constructed, although there will only be enough for 20% of those in need. The lucky ones will be decided by lottery. "Hello Work", a job finding agency, is making every effort to help those who lost their job or business to start again. And there are many, many meetings between government officials and the survivors who want to get their lives going once more. I watched one such gathering on TV. It was with farmers. Their strong, sturdy faces and weathered skin, their determination and conservative hold on life were a strong force full of potential for the future, given the opportunity. Rice planting season is coming soon. Farming is in those folks' blood, so they were holding a meeting to figure out what to do in the face of their tsunami-damaged, nuclear-threatened fields.

Japanese decisions are made by consensus. So in the discussion stage everyone is encouraged to speak. Rank does not play as strong a role as usual in this time of exploration. In fact, all ideas are respected and taken into account, no matter who presents them. In that particular meeting one simple farmer raised his hand and said, "We are ready for a vision. We want a step-by-step plan within a time frame so that we can 'gambaru', work hard, with a clear purpose. Otherwise our efforts will dissipate and be lost." Another said, "This is our low point. But we have to keep focusing on the future. If not, we won't go anywhere. Let's start making some specific plans."

The government officials listened. But since they try to take all viewpoints into account, decisions can take a very long time to be implemented. Also this particular situation -- the strongest quake on record in Japan, the monstrous tsunami, the nuclear problem, multiple daily quakes since then, tens of thousands of homeless, and thousands who lost their means of income – is the first of its kind here. So, there are no clear patterns to follow. But people are trying very hard to find a way.

But anger is starting to be expressed, too. The mayor of Kesennuma was in a meeting with executives of the Tokyo Electric Company. "Why are you doing this? Why are you trying to keep the nuclear facility going? You want electricity for Tokyo residents, but haven't you taken into consideration the incredible suffering you are causing us who live near the plant?" Such challenges towards authority seem very positive in light of the current tragedies.

Not surprisingly, as the roads start to open up and gasoline becomes more available, people are going to the devastated areas to have a look. They often take their children. "We want them to see this. We want the impact of this to be so deep they will never forget." Old-timers say people remember a big quake and tsunami for three generations. Then people have to learn all over again. There are signs everywhere here about the dangers of natural disasters and about where evacuation centers are. Kids are drilled from a very early age what to do in times of emergency. But without direct experience, the reality of those things seems like something out of a manga story. Adults want to make this current situation be so real their children and grandchildren will remember, and hopefully pass the awareness down beyond the third generation.

Individual stories are an important feature of the evening news here. Last night a woman was interviewed. She was staying at her boss's home. She had worked for him for fourteen years. When she lost her apartment to the tsunami, her boss felt an obligation to take her in, even though he, too, had lost much, including his factory. They both looked exhausted, as pretty much everyone does these days, and their main meal was cup ramen. "This is hard," she said. "But how can I complain? There are many others in the same situation as I am, or worse." She did not smile.

But there was another woman who did. She was called "Warai no Obaasan", The Smiling Grandmother. This woman was aged 93 and was always smiling. "Fortune favors those who smile," she said. "Even though I have lost my home and now live in a shelter, I smile. I want to help others to smile, too." So, she talks to everyone and tells funny stories or points out positive things, such as the increasing warmth of the days, the buds on the sakura trees, or the chance to take a weekly bath. She goes out for walks among the rubble of her town, looks at all the devastation and says, "We have to pull ourselves out of this. There is no other way. I am sure we can do it. We have to."

She herself had a remarkable past. In 1933, when she was 17, she experienced her first devastating tsunami. "I could find no words to express my sorrow," she reflected. "I lost my home, my friends, and my family. But locals helped me. Eventually I was able to open a small restaurant. That way I could support a few children orphaned by that tragedy. Later I had three of my own. We were all like one family.

"From that experience I learned that if we all work together, we will have hope. And if we have hope, we get energy and can do anything. Now we must smile to overcome what has befallen us. Yes, we must smile. And we cannot give up hope."

One big concern is the use of electricity. Tokyo already has rotating blackouts, but government officials want to do much more. They are talking about laws to limit the use of electricity and fines if they are broken. They are discussing the possibility of a rotating schedule for usage. For example, one section of the city may have company blackouts on Monday and Tuesday, while another may have them on Thursday and Friday.

Other options include starting work earlier when it is cooler, stopping work at 4:30 sharp, introducing day light savings, and working from home, which would reduce commuting. Already in some companies employees are encouraged to use the stairs, not elevators or escalators, at least when going down. Both companies and households are asked to unplug appliances when not in use, to reduce electrical usage in peak hours, and to place the refrigerator slightly away from the wall and raise the temperature inside by a few degrees. When really hot weather comes, men will not be expected to wear ties and suit jackets and woman can wear light slacks to avoid stockings. TV news is full of such suggestions for everyone to follow. Laws will soon follow.

Sendai has a baseball team called Rakuten. The team was away during the first quake, but came back to Sendai as soon as the roads were open. The manager divided the members into groups of four to visit the shelters. "We need to encourage the survivors, especially those who have lost everything. We need to remind them that tragedies are an opportunity to make us stronger. But we cannot give in to depression or despair. We must keep fighting. We must keep a positive spirit."

And all of us are trying very hard to do just that, even if it is "only" in the circumference of our own personal lives. But that little bit, we hope, will radiate out, giving strength and courage to all those in need.

Love,

Anne

LETTER TWENTY · BLOCK ISLANDERS
HELP JAPANESE ISLANDERS

Albeit a departure from Anne's letters, we felt it important to include a story that first appeared in the Block Island Times. A classic, New England setting and storied, maritime community, Block Island sits 13 miles off the coast of Rhode Island, in Anne's native USA. Written by Anne's cousin, Block Islander, Susan Brown Black, the following serves as heartwarming testament to the efforts of a comparatively tiny island coming together in its own, unique way to assist an island nation in its hour of need – half a world away. Most importantly, this exemplifies the profound ability of the simple acts of kindness that Anne reveals to inspire extraordinary compassion in individuals of all ages and persuasions, and entire communities alike – whose only affinity with a distant culture and people is to act as one on their behalf – in the very best spirit of humanity.

. . .

April 14, 2011

'Letters from Sendai'

by Sue Brown Black

Have you heard about the letters from Sendai, Japan? My cousin, Anne Thomas has been e-mailing one almost every day since the big earthquake and tsunami on March 11th. They have gone viral on the internet and are being read all over Block Island and around the world. Bruce Decker told me his wife received one of Anne's letters that was forwarded from a friend in Hong Kong.

Anne, who is 62, has spent the past 22 years living in Sendai, Japan and teaches English there. She grew up in Maryland and majored in art at URI, with minors in English and French. She received her Masters Degree in Education from George Washington University in DC. and her certificate to teach English as a Foreign Language from International House in London. Anne has spent her whole adult life traveling, teaching English in Colombia, The UK, France, Spain, Morocco, Indonesia, India, spending a few years in each country, learning about their cultures and religions. "Traveling, drawing, writing, ceaseless curiosity, and profound love of others are some of the ways I connect to my soul" Anne wrote. She did not stop moving until she landed in Japan and discovered its unique people and culture. I have learned about Japan from Anne's stories and cultural gifts we've received from her over the years.

I had the opportunity to team teach with Anne in an exchange between my daughter's sixth grade classroom and Anne's English students in Japan. We exchanged gifts, candy and videotapes of ourselves. It was an awesome experience for all of us and we learned a ton about their culture.

I was really excited to visit Anne in Japan when I joined my husband on his merchant ship last fall. It was a big disappointment when our cargo in Asia was cancelled because there is such a decreased need for Japanese cars with the current U.S. economy. Unfortunately, I missed a chance to visit Anne and who knows how long it will take before visitors can go to Sendai again with all the unsettling events they are experiencing as the earth adjusts herself.

Anne has posted 19 letters at the time of this writing. She describes her experiences during the aftermath of the earthquake in great detail. She gives us a different view and does a wonderful job teaching us about the goodness of the people of Japan. The letters are posted on a link at the Block Island Times' community website, Village Soup, at: www.blockislandtimes.com for everyone to read.

I have had many heartfelt responses from my friends who have read the letters. Here are few of them:

Jackie Brown wrote, "Reading these letters allows one to see beauty, kindness and love in the face of devastation."

Robin Burke wrote, "If ever there were words of compassion, these are them. She must be an angel."

Gail Ballard Hall wrote, "I'm overwhelmed by humanity, while these letters bring me to tears as I read them."

Ann Walsh wrote, "The letters really opened our eyes up to what is really precious in life and the strength of these people."

Judy Kisseberth wrote, "Anne's letters are an amazing synopsis of their reality and also very encouraging to know that everyone is looking out for one another. I find the Japanese culture so amazing."

Skip McAloon who lives in New Orleans wrote, "It is nice to hear from someone on the ground rather than the press. I recall that after Katrina if I wanted to know what was happening around here the LAST place I would go was the press. They sensationalize EVERYTHING in order to sell advertising, but they don't tell the real story. E-mails like your cousin's are the ones that give real information."

Ann's letters and the overall situation in Japan after the tragedy have inspired Block Islanders.

On Block Island there is a strong community effort to raise awareness, support and honor the people of Sendai. English teacher Nancy Greenaway's senior class students will recite Anne's letters for their public presentation this year. Judy Durden's third grade students who are doing a unit on Japan have written cards and will collect items like pencils and crayons to send. The future business leaders club have had bake sales to raise money. We're making plans for a large fundraiser also. Anne said that she loves the idea of a fundraiser and it would give her friends in Japan courage to know that people on the other side of the world are working to support them in their time of desperate need.

We decided on April 29th as the day to hold the fundraiser because it is a national holiday in Japan. It is the day they celebrate their Emperor. In Japan the day is normally spent having picnics under cherry blossom trees, flying carp streamers and enjoying family time and gathering together for the rice planting season. I'm sure it will be quite different for them this year.

Event coordinator Kate Musso, and others are helping to organize the event which will be held at the McGovern's Yellow Kittens in conjunction with their weekly Clam Shack. There will be a sushi contest, raw bar with clams and oysters and pot luck Asian food themed buffet. People may bring other food also. People with Japanese memorabilia, pictures, etc. are asked to bring things to be displayed. The third grade will loan decorations from their classroom for the event. Anne's letters will be printed for distribution and will have covers made by students chosen from a book cover contest. There will be before-and-after pictures of the tsunami, and Herman Hassinger might show a slide show of Japanese gardens and we might even have foot washings in the corner.

Kate Musso came up with the idea of becoming a sister city to Sendai and finding a non profit in Sendai similar to our local Mary D Fund to send donations to, instead of to just the larger organizations doing relief work. Anne has helped us find a fund started by Imai Sensei to help the homeless. His group is doing some the best local work in Sendai following the earthquake and tsunami, and we will send our donations there. You can Google him at odemagazine.com (now odewire.com) and see pictures on his website at www.yomawari.net. Anne wrote, "He is so cool and I admire him so much. A true saint who is not afraid to get his hands filthy working on behalf those who need it the most."

If you want to help, if you or someone you know makes sushi, if you can contribute some food to the fundraiser or prizes for the contest, if you have Japanese items for display, or can help in any other way, please get in touch through this paper.

The fundraiser will be held on Friday, April 29th from 4:30 to 6:30 so families with young children can attend early, and people participating in the Historical Preservation weekend kick off reception at the Harbor Church will have time to get there later. There will be a $10 (suggested minimum) donation to vote on the sushi contest and eat at the buffet, but admission to Clam Shack will be free.

If you can't attend the fundraiser and would like to make a tax deductible monetary donation, please send a check made payable to Block Island Ecumenical Ministries (BIEM) marked "Sendai" and mail it to:

Block Island Ecumenical Ministries (BIEM)
PO Box 277
Block Island, RI 02807 USA

Their group has kindly agreed to sponsor a Sendai Fund by acting as our host organization and sending all monies raised to relief efforts in Japan, as they do for other worthy causes. Mary Donnelly of BIEM said, "It's important for us to help those in need around the world, not just those on our island."

Thanks in advance for helping our island help our sister island in Japan. My sister's small town in Vermont has already raised

$3500. I'm sure we can at least match that!! Hope to see you all on the 29th.

Letter Twenty-One

April 15, 2011

Dear Family and Friends,

I thought my last letter would be my final one until after my move. But some people have asked me to kindly keep up these epistles. So since I will be off line for about a month starting Sunday, I realized I should get one more out before then. And very fortunately a friend sent me an e-mail, which expresses how many of us are feeling these days.

Steve and I used to work in the same university in Sendai. It was called Shokei. He hoped for full-time employment there, but the administration had other ideas. It was planning on eliminating the English Department completely, so not only would Steve not get a position, but I would soon lose my job there, too.

Steve knew he had to support his wife and child, so started to look elsewhere. That little family ended up in the UAE. Yuki, Steve's wife, comes from Iwaki, an area severely devastated by the recent natural catastrophes. Her father is a fire fighter there. And when all the hard work began after the quake, he worked 7/24 and ate two rice balls a day. He continues his total commitment, without holding anything back whatsoever. This is what Steve said about him in an e-mail of several weeks ago:

"I really really, super really, respect the father more than any living person right now. He is a hero – even with radiation his people are priority, even higher than family, but 'for' family. No attachment in the best possible way."

. . .

His tireless service was recognized. As Steve said in today's message:

"Yuki's father made the paper today for being a local hero – as we all thought he was. That's a nice reward, perhaps."

...

But what Steve said in the following e-mail seems to sum up the confusions we all are feeling here. There is so much beauty, but also so much destruction. So much hope, but fringes of despair. So much effort, but so much exhaustion. So much purposefulness, but so much uncertainty. We build and then another quake knocks all the repairs down. We clean up, yet are told another major quake will come within a month. We live each moment acutely aware, always praying for a day filled with the simple beauties of life, always alert to what can happen suddenly and at anytime, always grateful for life itself and that we are allowed to participate in it.

Here is Steve's letter in its entirety. It says the same things I just did, but better.

"Love being part of the letters, the lessons, the trials and tribulations.

"Yuki's family I feel is loosing hope. I fear. They clean, as you do, another quake comes and the restart the cleaning. House washed away and the parents' house that 'was fine' is now getting cracks in its walls with the 7.0+ aftershocks. They were optimistic. They are pessimistic. They were ready to face a challenge. They are having a hard go now.

"It is once again strange to hear about this from the 'outside'. I want to be there to help. I am happy not to be there. It is a very confusing time there and with the nuclear alert going from 5 to 6 to 7 there is even more reason to have concern and to not want to be in Iwaki, more reason to not want to be in Japan. Many what ifs play in my head. What if Shokei had kept me and what if we did move to Natori as we considered – and even found (a place to live there)? What if, what if, what if?

"I feel like a bad son-in-law as I am not there for family and a bad friend for not being there for friends. I want to help you. I want to find vegetables in small shops and look for the 2 kg bag of rice with you and sleep in my clothing to take-part in this event. I am also glad I am only writing about this desire. I am glad my wife and daughter are here (and) not exposed to the trauma that many are experiencing.

"It is good to read your letters and views as you are able to see the lessons life has to throw out. It sounds as if others are also able to see this as well, and this is the best sign. Not all can see this. I hear they even have a new word, 'flygin', for the mass numbers of gaijin (foreigners) leaving. I never thought I would have this day to reflect upon. I remember thinking about going to Tanzania (no clue about Japan), and then thinking about going to Japan (no clue again). I spent a short time there compared to you, just 7 years, but fell in love with the nation.

"It is very confusing thinking about Japan, like the frog coming out in July confused and dazed, I don't know how to look at this."

Kindest regards,

Steve

. . .

I guess for all of us, how we view and experience this will continue to evolve with time, perhaps for the rest of our lives.

Love,

Anne

. . .

For further insights and an update regarding Yuki's father and his heroic efforts, please also see Response Nineteen (pages 189-190) – Steve Pellerine's wonderful follow-up to Anne's Letter Twenty-One.

LETTER TWENTY-TWO

May 17, 2011

(This letter was written over several weeks when I was off line. Another such will follow soon.)

...

Dear Family and Friends,

It has been well over a month since I have been in touch. Much has happened in that time, both in Japan and in my personal life. Of course, the world's attention has mostly sifted away from the disasters here, but even so, there is a lot still going on. This country has been slowly and steadily getting back on her feet. Progress is uneven, but it is happening everywhere. Extremely devastated areas are still struggling with clean up and rebuilding, but much effort has been made to get Sendai proper functioning as normally as possible. We still have ongoing daily earthquakes, huge cracks in the roads, shattered buildings and walls, and protective blue mats everywhere, but reconstruction work is evident wherever you look. Supermarkets are open normal hours now and are well stocked, although some items are still unavailable or rationed. Almost everyone is intensely focused on remaking their lives. Those who were seriously hit have had to start almost from scratch, but even those who suffered little physical loss are trying to reassess their attitudes, values, and ways of being in the world. Almost everyone is caught up in a wave of discarding unneeded items, and rearranging material belongings to reflect the deep inner changes that this searing tragedy has brought about. A former student of mine, who now lives in Singapore, came to Sendai to help her parents. As she sorts through her family home, she keeps asking her mother, "Do you really need this anymore? Why not get rid of it? Why not start again fresh?" Another student has taken load after load of earthquake-broken or unneeded items to the dump. She was totally astonished to see the mountains of goods that people are getting rid of. But the rubbish place is well organized, typical for Japan. "TVs go over there, refrigerators on that pile, heavy dressers are down this row and on the left," say the guards at the entrance. Yes, it is a time of peeling away, discarding, reassessing needs and wants.

But there is a lot of buying, too. Home centers, for example, are packed with people sorting through furniture, appliances, bedding, and carpets. There is not an "S" hook to be found in most hardware stores, as people are buying them by the fists-full to hang things in their newly arranged homes. Companies are all displaying messages that say: "We apologize to you for not being able to serve you for several weeks after the recent disaster. That was very inconvenient for you, so please allow us to give you a discount on our items." Or they might say, "We have all suffered a great deal in the past few months. So, please refresh your feelings by the generous prices we are offering in our shops."

The first week in May is called Golden Week. That is because there is a series of national holidays one after another. That is the time famous carp streamers are hung out in honor of children. You can see them flapping everywhere this year, more so than usual: above buildings, across roads, in people's gardens, even over rubble. They bring a great sense of hope and of joy. This week traditionally people travel for enjoyment, very often overseas. But this year most people from this area feel a need to stay close to their roots; or they are too busy sorting out their personal lives. So instead of going to other places, the big trend now is to volunteer. Locals are, of course. But other people are, too. Rather than going overseas, people from all over the country are flocking to this area to lend a hand. Sendai Station has a booth with a list of places needing volunteer services. The city hall has a bulletin board with the same kind of information. In fact, dotted all over this area there are centers recruiting volunteers of all sorts. No matter what people's specialty, everyone wants to contribute in some way. The sense of drive and of purpose is palpable everywhere. One young woman friend loves to make cakes. So she has been making almost 700 bean cup cakes on her days off and has them delivered to evacuation centers, where there are still hundreds of people waiting their turn to get a temporary home. And signs all over town say: "Gambatte Miyagi! Gambatte Sendai!" This adds to the enthusiasm and drive to rebuild, to forge ahead without giving up, no matter how daunting the work involved may be.

Sports are really big now, too. They provide an energetic diversion from tragedy and also promote a sense of team spirit and working together for success. There have been several baseball games in the past few weeks. Usually Sendai's team plays with great élan, but always loses. This past week, however, it has been winning every game, to the cheers of the astonished and delighted crowd.

But for some people things move on a much deeper level. A friend, who lives in hard-hit Natori, came to Sendai to help me with changing legal documents after my move. She told me that normally she loved coming to the city; she appreciated the variety and stimulus of Sendai. But now all she wants to do is to be quiet and reflective at home. Previously she had volunteered for two days in evacuation shelters, where her job was to register people. But after hearing story after story of dead or missing relatives, and not knowing what to say or how to comfort the victims, she realized that sort of work was too emotionally overwhelming for her. The depth and extent of this traumatic event hit her very hard. She told me that now it was difficult for her to focus. She reads my letters or news articles, understands every word, but can not pull the ideas together to make coherent sense. So for her, as for many, this upheaval has created a time of deep soul searching and wonder.

Actually, I have found a similar attitude in my own life. It is very hard to be other than nose-to-nose with the present moment. Life is the Now. And that is more than enough. Also the circumference of my efforts has narrowed considerably because of having to move. And when I relocated into this new apartment, I realized immediately that this would take all my time and energy. I sensed, too, that I wanted to be fully attentive to what was happening in my own life, even though I am still greatly concerned with what is happening to others all around me. One small way to honor my desire to be attentive was that I did not turn on music I love, catch up on reading, or listen to the news, as I would normally do. I found those activities too intrusive and inappropriate. Rather I wanted to be totally receptive to this place and myself in it. I wanted this new home to speak to me, rather than actively fill it with my former self. So I have spent days in silence, with "only" the sound of birds, wind, and rain, with "only" the prismatic sunlight that graciously illumines these rooms, with "only" an inner attunement of how to arrange this new home to reflect the person I am now. It has been an exhausting, but very sacred time for me. I realize that starting over like this occurs very rarely. So I have been making it be a privilege, one that I am fully attuned to while it is happening, not as William Wordsworth would say in moments of tranquility and reflection after the fact.

I do not have a TV, but the other day I stopped by my favorite greengrocer's, where Grandma was watching the local news. She and I sat next to each other, watching, commenting on the sadness of it all. There are literally thousands still in shelters, many are sick from lack of exercise and from sleeping on hard cold floors. It is especially hard on the old, of course, but small children find it very confusing, too, especially if they have lost one parent or both. For many this is truly a period of "Gaman" or "Gambatte": "Don't give up." "Hang in there." "Keep up the fighting spirit."

A friend told me that every night on TV the local news follows the story of one family. It shows the devastation, presents the tremendous loss, but always tries to balance that in favor of individuals' positive spirit, their determination to begin again and to get life moving forward in a constructive manner. Even though in many ways it seems as if people are trying to go back to how things were before – factories running smoothly, products available in stores, people concerned about appearance – in reality no one is the same. People may strive for outer things to appear as they were before, but the inner dimension is entirely different from when March 11 changed our lives forever.

My friend also described the tremendous effort people are making to coordinate children still in shelters with specific schools. They are trying to arrange it so that children can return to school with former classmates. Some youngsters have been relocated very far from this area, however, and unfortunately sometimes their new classmates will bully them, saying, "You have 'radiation coodies.' We don't want you here." So, it can be an extra long, up hill struggle for some. But even so, every effort is being made to help the children and their families. Kobe was hard hit with an earthquake several years ago. So, the local Tohoku governments have invited children from there to come to this area to encourage the kids here. Many of those youngsters also lost parents, so know the terrible consequences of this sort of natural disaster. In one shelter all the children, from both Kobe and Tohoku, held hands making a circle. They swayed and sang together, giving each other love and understanding. At other times those lovely kids from far away would read to elementary school children still in shelters. And then they would do various activities together. All these are little steps that, hopefully, someday will bring about an all-encompassing level of healing.

Other work of volunteers, adults, is to sort through the debris and collect various items of importance. A picture album here, a bracelet there, a shoulder bag or a fragile bowl: all the little things that make up ordinary daily life. Then they take these precious items to a central area, where the evacuees can sort through them, and hopefully find something that is theirs and that holds a universe of memories. Little acts of kindness, stemming directly from the heart, can make such a world of difference. In one extremely devastated area I saw the frame of a house still standing amid vast expanses of rubble. I was deeply touched to see one window still in tact and sitting on the sill were piles of books. Obviously the army clean-up crew had found these meaning-filled items and had graciously placed them where a family member, should they be able to return, would be able to find them. The cleaning up process is painfully slow precisely because the workers are doing it with deep consideration for the feelings of the victims. That is so much more important than a quick, efficient clean up. And also it is a very Japanese way of being in the world: thoughtfulness towards others' feelings.

There is a sense of caution in the air, but even so people are getting out and trying to enjoy life once again. In late April Izumi's family and I went out to the countryside to picnic under thousands of cherry trees in full bloom along a riverbank. We wandered slowly, savoring the gentle beauty all around. There were many others there, too. Usually there is a lot of drinking and merrymaking as people view the cherry blossoms. But this year the mood was different. There was no loud partying, no drunkenness, only a sense of deep appreciation. In fact, the atmosphere was subdued and solemn.

To get there we had to pass through Natori City, where we saw cars still lying in rivers, houses broken like splinters on the streets, and protective blue mats holding down walls or roofs of buildings. Even though we had seen such sights in our own neighborhood and every night on TV, it was a shock to see so much damage in such a concentrated area. We enjoyed the cherry trees, of course, but we also stayed constantly aware of the ongoing tragedy all around us.

The other day a friend and I were talking about national flowers and birds. Everyone knows the sakura, the cherry blossom, is Japan's flower. But did you know that the blue-black, screeching, forceful crow is her bird? I was totally amazed when I learned that curious fact. But when I thought about it, I could catch a wider understanding of the Japanese psychological and emotional makeup. Ethereal, very short-lived delicacy on the one side, and strong, focused, tenacious determination on the other. People here try to live balancing an attitude that honors those extremely divergent dimensions -- and everything in between. The Japanese are masters at temporarily diverting their attention away from their problems in order to appreciate a moment of beauty or pleasure. They do this not as a way to avoid their burdens or responsibilities, but as a way to live a balanced life. They fully enjoy a happy moment, knowing they will soon return to their work, hopefully refreshed and ready to put all their efforts once again into what is demanded of them.

This message is getting very long, so I would like to end with a quotation that I came across as I was sorting through my papers. I have no idea where it comes from, but that does not detract from the message. "In his beautiful book, *Man's Search for Meaning,* Viktor Frankl, the Jewish psychiatrist who is also a concentration camp survivor, writes: 'A man who becomes conscious of the responsibility he bears towards a human being who affectionately waits for him, or to an unfinished work, will never be able to throw away his life. He knows the "why" for his existence, and will be able to bear almost any "how".' "

That seems to sum up much of what is happening here now. Most Japanese who are currently facing a life filled with sorrow and loss also have a tremendous sense of unfinished work. As one man said, "I want to rebuild not for myself but for the children." That forward-looking attitude, so much larger than oneself, is a motivating factor uniting us all.

Love,

Anne

LETTER TWENTY-THREE

May 20, 2011

Dear Family and Friends,

Please forgive this letter, which will be mostly about myself. My move has totally absorbed all my focus and energy for the past few weeks. So, that is about all I have to share with you at this time. I apologize for the narrowness of this indulgence.

I am very fortunate in that work had not yet begun whilst I was involved in the significant task of moving, so I could give myself over fully to that enjoyable, but demanding task of evolving this place into a home. Actually, I realized I had never really done this before. At least not in this way. I have moved often, but each time I resettled, I was given hand-me-down furniture and furnishings. So my homes have been hodgepodge at best, very dumpy at worst. But this time the rumbling, jerking earth did an amazing amount of damage to my furniture; or maybe everything was so old that one piece after another succumbed to its own inner rot and pre-earthquake brokenness. Whichever, I find I have had to refurbish my home with new things this time. Mostly shelves, lots of them. But also a table and a chair, and various other odds and ends that hold a home together. This process of thinking about what would make pleasant living space and going out to find it has been an interesting involvement and observation for me.

The moving itself was quite an experience. One professional moving company refused to enter my old shack to help me; they found it too dangerous to step foot inside. But fortunately, another was less exacting. Plus eleven energetic friends kindly came to the rescue. Between all of us lugging boxes down a narrow lane to the waiting cars and then squeezing ourselves one after another through the small entranceway of this apartment, we managed to get all of me from there to here in less than three hours. Then we sat amid boxes and books to enjoy a lunch of huge rice balls and jello made by my loving helpers.

For about ten days afterwards I purchased and assembled bookshelves, arranged my still-too-many belongings neatly, and realized I would have to cover the one room of "western flooring" before I scratched and marked the lovely wood beyond repair. I bought tatami matting for that floor, so now I am more traditional all through this place. (The other two rooms have tatami.) In fact, when the tottering old landlord met me, he said, "I heard you wanted tatami, so I knew it would be all right to rent to this foreigner. You are the first, so we were not sure."

A former student took me to a home center to make these floor purchases. I have a terrible time making up my mind with things involving measurements, but felt pressure to get this finished before classes began, making my time no longer be my own. When I mentioned that to my student, she said, "Anne Sensei, I have never heard you sound like an American before. Don't rush things. Take your time and get what you really want. We can always come back another time."

The real estate agent, when I asked him if this place were safe, responded with earthquakes in mind. I was thinking more of thieves since this apartment is on the first floor, tucked back. I never worried about that sort of thing in my old shack. It was in a neighborhood in which everyone had known each other for generations. I usually left the door unlocked and the postman would sometimes reach in and put my mail directly on the table. But here is different. It is an apartment complex, so there is less a sense of continuity. When the real estate agent realized my meaning of theft, not earthquakes, he carefully explained that break-ins here take about three minutes: one to cut the glass near the lock, one to flip the lock and enter, one to snatch and depart. Since everyone here lives very close together, people tend not to smash glass, as it would make too much noise and alert the neighbors. So the landlord had installed a very simple device to lock the sliding doors in two places, making a fast entry and exit virtually impossible. I felt relieved. Having my flat next to the landlord's daughter's makes me feel safer, too. I have not thought about this sort of thing since moving to Japan, where life is very safe compared to other places in the world. But my instincts go into alert when I am faced with a new situation, so I asked just to be sure.

I wake up each day and wonder, "What new thing will I learn today?" "What does today have to teach me?" And I find every day does indeed reveal unexpected bits of wisdom. I sprained my elbow assembling my bookcases, for example, and when I went for a massage, the man told me to use my baby and ring fingers for gripping, not the middle or index. "If you can learn how to use your hands that way, you will never get tennis elbow again. You know how the Yakusa sometimes have their baby fingers cut off? When they lose a fight, the winner will cut off their opponent's source of power, the baby finger. And those are the fingers I use when I do kendo. You can get a lot of power that way." I am still trying to master this skill. I am not there yet, but I can definitely feel a difference in my arms from my efforts to retrain myself in this manner.

I have also learned how important it is to place everything low down. I used to have tall shelves, but they crashed when the big quakes hit. So, now all my bookcases and kitchen shelves are waist high, no more. Also I noticed in a nearby hospital that all the TVs are now on the floor, not high up. They were also tied securely to the wall. Shops still have survival items for sale in prominent places: wide tape, heavy-duty string, strong flashlights, and small camping stoves. All are much needed items these days. We know another big quake could easily come anytime. In fact, we have been told the "danger" time for another major quake is one year.

I have learned lots of other practical things, too. For example, Izumi taught me to leave my futons open while I eat breakfast. That way they have a chance to cool and will not mold when folded up in the closets. This building is made of steel, not wood, so does not breathe like my old house did. Mold will be a constant challenge here, she warned me.

She also taught me that there are various sizes of tatami rooms. They are sized by "jo". Old sizes are bigger than new, even though both have the same number of "jo". Plus hotels and restaurants have a different, even larger size, although the numbers are also the same. A good lesson in relativity, which is fundamental to the Japanese way of being in the world. Fortunately my apartment is old by Japanese standards, but well refurbished, so I have a bit more room than I would if I were in a very modern place. It is in my genes to have my home bulging with items of love and beauty, so I am very grateful for the few centimeters of extra space. I appreciate, but do not live in Japanese wabi.

Another friend told me to immediately wash my new tatami with warm water. "You must ring the warm water out of a rag and then rub down each mat several times. There is a lot of dust and bits of grass in new tatami," he explained. "So it is important to get them very clean before you start using them."

From the window of my new place I can see a small cedar forest. I was told that those tall dark trees, which now cover many parts of this country, were introduced by the Americans after World War II. They were a perfect solution to the housing problem. Their tall, arrow-straight trunks were good for beams and uprights of wooden homes.

I have learned from this experience that appropriate moving gifts are ones that are very practical. I was very fortunate and grateful to receive liquid hand soap, packaged food of all sorts, hand cream, and a pump that sucks water out of my bathtub into the washing machine so as not to waste water. Gift giving is part of the fabric of this culture. So much so that there are set times for expressing gratitude via reciprocal presents: mid-summer and at the end of the year. And giving is indeed tit-for-tat. So in June I will follow the national tradition of sending Thank-You-In-Return gifts to everyone who has helped me so far this year. I will probably send fish, noodles, or fruit.

In the past few years the local government has been consolidating villages into larger political units. And as they do so, they have been sweeping away the names of places, absorbing them into larger cities. This obliteration of names is seen as practical and efficient. However, recent events are revealing the wisdom of the old. One place where hundreds of people were swept away in a matter of minutes was called "Arahama". That translates as "Rough Beach". Realizing the perfect match of that name and the recent tragedy there, authorities were reminded that the traditional names actually described what a locale was like. And as in the case of "Arahama", they served as a warning for possible disaster. If people had paid attention to that name, they may not have built their homes, businesses, and farms there. So now they are beginning to question the renaming of places. Even though old names may be less efficient administratively, in the long run, they may prove to be a better choice.

Another thing I have witnessed is that for the average mature Japanese the pursuit of happiness is not a fundamental driving force, as it is in some cultures. Rather in this country the ideal seems to be to accept life's challenges without complaint and to work hard dealing with them, and possibly, if you are lucky, some day to overcome them. It seems that for most Japanese deep satisfaction from strong endeavor is far more important and respected than one's own personal happiness.

And yet, there is a very deep appreciation of beauty here. Also people's feelings matter a great deal. Often business transactions of any sort start with a bit of chitchat to make the atmosphere pleasant. The other day, for example, when a large, muscular delivery man came to my home, I greeted him by saying what a lovely day it was. He agreed and added that it was a real pleasure to be delivering goods that day because he could enjoy all the flowers in people's gardens and the few cherry blossoms that were still holding on. I smiled at the Japanese flavor of his sensitivity, which being so innate to him, he was completely unaware of.

I have found it fascinating watching myself and others shift out of pure survival mode. The first change I noticed in others was in fashion. Some young women went right back to their trendy clothes of micro-mini skirts and spiked heels. I was startled at first, because their flimsy, overly revealing outfits seemed totally out of place. But a friend said it might be their way to get back to normal life as quickly as possible. Yet, I wonder why they chose to do so by going back to how they were before instead of moving forward into something that more closely reflected their new selves. With adults it is different, of course. With them outer appearance seems less crucial. Instead I sense a relief and appreciation that daily life is slowly getting back to normal.

Personal post-survival changes are many. The first after I moved was to wash my hair more often. Plus I started sleeping in pajamas instead of in street clothes. And then I got a haircut. My hands have become torn and very tough from all the packing, unpacking, building and arranging. So, I have started using creams and wearing gloves even when I am not hard at work. I also change my clothes daily now. And I take the time to cook full meals and to actually sit down to eat them. I hand write letters (until I got Internet connection). And I do stretching exercises each morning rather than leaping out of bed with my mind bursting with things to do.

I have not started to read yet, however. But I can feel myself becoming ready for T'ai Chi classes again. Most high ceilings collapsed with the violent shaking, so we are waiting for a place to open up where lessons can be held. And my drawing is less frantic, less a way to keep me from going mad. Even these generic letters, which at first were the glue that held me together and helped give shape to what was happening, are no longer the center of my focus. They help record my observations and feelings, but are no longer a desperate need.

Probably most importantly I have relearned -- acutely -- how crucial friends are. My individualistic childhood culture admires people who "go it alone", who make decisions for themselves, and who are independent. There is great pride in that pioneer-like mentality. There is much good in that, of course. But here in this collective culture of admitted dependency, people realize survival and the quality of life depend on connection to others. During all the upheavals of this time, I realize that without the love and support of friends, I would have been very desperate indeed. Five weeks as a welcomed member of Izumi's household, all of the generous friends who helped me move, (including my old neighbor who at first was annoyed that so many were traipsing past his gorgeous garden, but who finally brought out his beloved red wheelbarrow for us to haul my many bundles of books), who took me to home centers to refurbish my apartment, and who accompanied me to government offices to register address changes, the smiles and support of the oldsters in my former neighborhood, and the kindness of the folks in this apartment complex – all are part of the fabric of this monumental experience. And without those wonderful people, where would I be? Indeed, who would I be?

Next week classes in the university start. And then my energy and focus will shift once again. This luxury, albeit exhausting, of time to reflect and to deliberately recreate my life without interruption will be over and I, too, will plunge back into "normal" life once again. I am growing eager to meet my students, to hear their stories and tell them mine. And I am very curious to see how things will be different with them, who are 18 and 19 years old – and how much will be the same.

Love,

Anne

LETTER TWENTY-FOUR

May 23, 2011

Dear Family and Friends,

The other day my friend Junko came rushing into my apartment. She was all excited and said, "Listen to what happened to me. I just went to get a massage. You know how much trouble I have been having ever since I started washing all those jars and cans after the tsunami. I have had to do that sort of hard work for my company for about a month now and it is awful! And my body is a real mess. When I was there getting a massage, they put glass ball suction cups on me to try and get the blood moving in certain very painful parts of my body. But when they did that, the whole area because grossly purple. The purple part is normal but mine was almost black it was so purple. Sasaki Sensei went to get 'Papa' (the boss) to ask for his advice."

"Papa" is a seer. He can see spirits around people. Not everyone has them, but when they do and when the spirits cause trouble, "Papa" tries to help.

"You have a spirit clinging to you," he told Junko. Then he began to massage her painful arm very gently and to chant a Buddhist prayer, calling Jiso San to come and take the desperate child away. When he had finished, Junko felt so much lighter, as if a huge weight had been lifted from her.

When she talked to me, she was both astonished and glad. Astonished that the soul of a recently deceased child had clung to her for help. When Junko began the clean-up job after the tsunami, she kept having dreams of drowning, and of desperate attempts to escape. "Papa" told her that she was very sensitive to the world of spirits, so they were turning to her in their desperation. Junko called herself "an easy target" for them. So, she was glad to finally be rid of this spirit who had been pulling at her for weeks.

However, as I listened to her, my reaction was a bit different. For me this was not a time to view this soul's attachment as a bad thing. From what Junko had told me, it seemed this particular soul was of a small child who had died in the tsunami. It was obviously confused. I remember reading something that Edgar Cayce once said. He pointed out that when souls die unexpectedly, in an accident for example, for a while they often do not realize that they have died. They are very confused as they wander in a state between earthly life and timelessness. So for me rather than look with horror upon what was happening, it was more a time of deep responsibility towards the child who was clinging to her.

"Junko, why not pray for the child? If you brush her away, she will only try to find someone else to cling to. If she comes to you again, then talk to her. Tell her that she is no longer alive on earth. Tell her to turn around and see angels. They are there to help her and to show her the way to heaven. Don't let your own ego get involved in this. You seem to be more sensitive than others, so you have the responsibility to do something positive for those who come to you for help."

And it seems others feel as I do. A few days after Junko came to my apartment, she and I went to Sendai Airport and Arahama. Even though more than two months have passed since the first major earthquake and tsunami, the devastation was still unbelievable. There are mountains of crushed cars and rubble from broken homes, vast expanses of leveled villages and farms, paddies flooded with salt water, a strange odor of burnt metal, and a pervading sense of desolation and deep sadness. Yet in among the jumble of desolation there was a tiny makeshift altar where a child's body had been found. That place of respect had plastic flowers, stuffed toys, one small shoe, and a Jiso statue holding its hands in silent prayer.

Later I read in the newspaper that an 82-year-old flute aficionado named Watanabe Kyoichi and his wife Ruiko had been missing since this tragedy began. People who loved them and adored their music went to the site of their home, now a pile of rubble, and gave a kocarina wooden flute concert there. They played for the souls of those two musicians whom they respected and honored. Everyone knew that the concert itself, played from the depths of the heart, connected all those concerned with love, whether they were physically alive or not.

No one can be fully sure of spirit entities. Some believe, some do not. Some have seen or sensed them, some have not. But I do know that even now the cries of the deceased can be heard everywhere. They are in the wail of the crows, the sighing of the wind, and the pattering of the rain. The earth itself very deeply resonates with silence and sadness. There is an underlying sense of profound tragedy everywhere, even though we all are soldiering on with our lives.

Last week classes began again in the prestigious women's university where I teach. The students are putting on the usual show of the latest outfits and make-up, the most trendy struts and gestures. But even so, there is something that runs much deeper. Faces are drawn, cheeks are hollow, eyes are framed by dark circles. We have all lost something. Yes, we have been through hell, and some are still in it. Some are dealing better than others, some having a harder time. But I am glad to once more be back with young, eager minds. I love their openness to life, their dreams for the future, and their exploration of what it means to be blossoming into adulthood. This school year will be positive, I trust, because we are all working for a more stable life and a better world together.

Love,

Anne

LETTER TWENTY-FIVE

May 28, 2011

Dear Family and Friends,

This will probably be my last letter in this series. I want to end these correspondences with a report written by my friend Imai Sensei, a Baptist preacher who runs a homeless center here in Sendai. He has also been helping victims of the recent earthquake and tsunami. He is my hero through and through. Recently he asked me to edit an article he was sending out to his friends in various countries. He gave me permission to send it along to you. It gives a very vivid picture of what has been going on here even now and his very admirable work for those severely affected by the recent disasters.

. . .

"'The kingdom of God exists within you' – and in the place of the great Japanese earthquake disaster."

– Seiji IMAI

Associate Professor, Shokei Gakuin University
President, Sendai Yomawari Group

"God, our Lord, the Creator of heaven and earth, even now you rule history". That was a normal salutation to God, which I said in my liturgy in Sendai-South Baptist Church on the morning of 27 March. To be honest, for a while after the earthquake I could not begin with this salutation. In a time of such terrible events, it is not easy to say something with God as the subject.

"On 11 March 2011 at 14:46 clock I was on the telephone with the District Land Transport Bureau in Aomori (North Tohoku). We were consulting about a former homeless person at our shelter on the matter of scrapping his car. At that very moment I was surprised by a great earthquake. Fortunately, our shelter in Sendai is far from the coast, where the earthquake originated. After several seconds, my friend on the other end of the telephone line informed me that the earthquake had just struck there, too. That was when I realized that the southern half of the Tohoku region was closer to the epicenter. As I ran to the entrance of our shelter to open the door to escape, the old building shook violently from side to side. Everything was swinging both vertically and horizontally, as if we were sitting on a tiny boat in the middle of the raging sea. Before my eyes, cracks went through the walls of the house. It looked like a scene from a movie. Then I immediately started to fill the bathtub with water to ensure drinking water. Even at that point in time the tap water was muddy and water was spouting out from a manhole cover like a fountain.

"After the main earthquake, which lasted quite a while, we hurried to ensure the safety of the residents of the house. I then instructed everyone to watch out for falling objects, and not to go outside immediately, because of aftershocks. I said, "If a strong earthquake should occur again, I cannot guarantee the security of the house". Then I told them to seek refuge in the nearest school building. We were also very concerned about another homeless shelter in a coastal area, in which many disabled people lived. But an employee had rushed there immediately and had found that everyone was safe. At that time we knew of the tsunami, but we believed that it would not affect us. We did not know that just two kilometers away from this shelter all hell had broken loose. In the evening I chatted by Skype on my battery-charged iPhone with Ms. Aoyama in Tokyo, whom I had met last year on the way back from

Germany via Siberia to Japan. I asked her to take care of my son, who had been on his way to Tokyo for the university entrance examination when the great earthquake happened. I could not make contact with him and was very worried. It was only then, as I talked with Ms. Aoyama, I learned that something very terrible had happened in the coastal area of the city of Sendai, and around the Sendai Airport.

"On Ustream of my iPhone and over the hand-generated-power-radio, I at least got minimal information, even if only in fragments. Because the electricity was cut off in the whole city of Sendai, I could not immediately see images on TV of the coastal area after the great tsunami. The next morning I went to a homeless shelter near the coastal area to deliver food and gas bottles. All roads to the coast were blocked. So I had to wait several days before I could see with my own eyes the place of the terrible disaster.

"When I went in an area behind the highway-dam on the side toward the sea, horrible scenes that I had never seen before were spread out before me. The eastern coastal area of the Wakabayashi district of Sendai was completely devastated. The tsunami had pounded over the pine forest and palisades and swept away houses and cars. Rubble from them was piled up under the bridge of the East Highway, which functioned as a dike and the last stronghold against the tsunami. I found sleeping bags besides the scrapped cars. Then I knew that the homeless who had lived in cars on the coast and along the dike had fallen victim to the raging tsunami. Other people who were living in cars and who were still alive were not counted in the homeless census by the Ministry of Health, Labor and Welfare (MHLW). It was the same for Internet cafe refugees. The fact that they are not counted in the census means that they are not qualified as beneficiaries of government support.

"Immediately after the earthquake, as strong aftershocks continued, we were commissioned by a social welfare office in the city of Sendai, to support a person living in a car who had narrowly escaped the tsunami. Until the tsunami he had parked his car on the coast and had lived there. But fortunately for him, he could no longer endure life in the car and was in the city for consultation at the time of the earthquake. If he had not done so, he would certainly have been a tsunami victim.

"As far as we know, many, many people who had lived on boats, in cars, or on the beach were wiped out by the tsunami. If we could have helped those individuals more positively before the disaster, or if MHLW had different principles allowing them to take more effective measures, those people might be alive today. It hurts us deeply in our souls when we think about what could have been. From this we can sadly say that there were various human causes besides the lack of evacuation systems and the nuclear accident in Fukushima that increased the number of victims in this disaster.

"The day after the earthquake, the first thing we did was to establish the safety of all of the residents in our homeless shelters and to ensure water and food for the moment. After that I went with Pastor Yasuhiro Aoki of the Sendai-South Baptist Church, who is also the Secretary General of Sendai Yomawari Group, to the administrative office of the Wakabayashi district. We wanted to give information about our situation so that we could distribute our stock and cook rice for the people stricken by the disaster. To give food for the hungry is indeed our normal service. Fortunately, our office uses propane gas, and miraculously had been spared from water supply interruption. Therefore, we could provide food for a hundred people immediately after the earthquake, even though the electric power was out.

"But total chaos prevailed in the administrative office of the district, and command structures there were all conflicting. Having been sent from one counter to another, we realized that no one knew what was going on or whom to ask. Finally, someone said: "Please go to the education advisory board, which is in the next building. There is a volunteer center there set up for disaster relief." However, even within 24 hours after the disaster, the volunteer center was not in operation. Emergency supplies had already been transported into the building, but the system of distribution was not yet working. The food had been simply piled up, so the evacuees in the administration building could not eat on a regular basis.

"So we came up with a very simple plan. "If the authorities do not offer cooked rice, we will make it ourselves. We would like to give something back to citizens who have supported us. In any case, let's cook and distribute rice until we use up the stock.""

"That is how "Curry-Rice-Run" began in front of our office and our church. At that time no one thought that this action would continue every day for two weeks, until the planned move of the office at the end of March. We let people know of our food program in local evening newspapers and on Twitter. "Free distribution of cooked rice, from 11:00 am to 13:00 clock in front of the office of the Sendai Yomawari Group, 17-25 Bunkamachi, Wakabayashi-Ku, while supplies last!" My messages on Twitter were immediately re-Tweeted, sometimes as many as 60 times per hour. Of course we provided rice even on rainy days and snowy days.

"When we ourselves could not distribute supplies, because of the church service on Sunday mornings, young people sent from the Volunteer Center cooked rice and handed out cans of food. Each day we handed out everything we had: curry rice, pork soup, clam chowder, chicken ramen, canned goods and so on. New contributors and donors, not only of food, came again and again.

We gave all the items that they delivered (such as food, clothing, sanitary items, and diapers) to the people coming to our office. The people who had been homeless even before the disaster were ready to help with the distribution of the cooked rice, and also to help the newly homeless citizens by giving them lots of support.

"Only now I can tell you that at the beginning we did not have enough stock to feed so many people for so long. We were taking a big chance, but we felt we had to do it. Many homeless people already lived in our shelter. And in order not to interrupt our charity work, we needed to ensure food primarily for employees and their families. If we did not do that, it would the death of our organization. But this extreme emergency situation was calling us to take reckless action. And when we did, we had various positive chain reactions.

"Thanks to their generosity many people manifested this magnificent truth: "It is more blessed to give than to receive" (Acts 20:35). For example one unknown citizen gave us a valuable gas bottle she had bought after hours of waiting time. She had stood in a long line since early morning to get it. Also pastors and church members of the Regional Association of Baptists in North Kanto delivered supplies several times and gave us assistance in distributing the cooked rice. They did this even in the earlier stages, before the situation of the nuclear power plants in Fukushima had been firmly established and so no one realized the danger of going through that affected area.

"At first we could not talk about God. It was not possible at all even to call upon God. We were too focused on the here and now. Our lifeline to the rest of the world had been cut off and no one knew when it would be restored. Nevertheless, we were able to do very practical things, like providing food for many people after the earthquake. The people were helpless, like sheep without a shepherd. And we kept reminding ourselves that Jesus of Nazareth, despite the refutation of his disciples (Mk 6:37), had dared the distribution of food with only five loaves and two fishes (V.41). We realized it was exactly the same with our twelve years of supporting the homeless and with the dire situation after the tsunami. We knew in the depths of our hearts that we were following Jesus of Nazareth. "Give us today the bread we need." (Matthew 6:11) "The kingdom of God exists within you." (Luke 17:21) Surely now we could hear the cry of Jesus, which has survived over eons of time and is still very much alive.

"As you read this report, the lifeline to basic services will have been restored in many places. But there are huge differences between the parties concerned, depending on whether they were directly affected by the tsunami or not. Attitudes towards work, courage, and time to rebuild are as different between people as heaven from earth. We still have a long road ahead for full recovery and reconstruction. The media will leave here and then no story on the disaster will be reported on TV. But we are still in need of your help. Please notice this, pray, and continue your active help! We need you, dear readers, for further assistance in the ongoing work that lies ahead. Thank you."

– Seiji IMAI

. . .

As I suggested in a past letter, if you would like to donate to help support Imai Sensei's work, please visit: www.yomawari.net.

Thank you.

Love,

Anne

124

LETTER TWENTY-SIX

June 26, 2011

Dear Family and Friends,

The past three months have been as if from a different dimension, a different consciousness, a different world entirely. The world's focus has shifted from us, but we are still shuffling along, picking up pieces one at a time, slowly moving back into the flow of life. An amazing time – and place – to be alive.

Life in Sendai proper is moving quickly back to appearing normal. Streets are being repaired, buildings reconstructed, stores reopened. Shops are well stocked; shoppers are plentiful. People are concerned about fashion and looking good once again. Under the surface, however, there is still much to be done. Water is not rationed, but we are being reminded to conserve. (Wash dishes in a bowl of water, turn off the shower as you scrub, don't let the water run continuously as you wash your face.) Electricity, too, is a very precious commodity. (Don't use the air conditioner unless absolutely needed. Men can go to work in short sleeved shirts and no jacket, women in loose skirts with knee high stockings.) Rules and regulations in this formal society are flexible if the situation calls for it. Basic survival over the long haul is a constant concern for everyone now.

Even though Sendai herself is standing straighter and prouder these days, much is still calling to be done. The areas towards the sea are still in shambles. The relief and clean up work is continuing slowly. But the time to bulldoze over the mounds of stinking debris has not yet arrived. Just recently a cluster of bodies was found bogged down in a huge pool of mud. The corpses had disintegrated, so the victims were identified by their teeth.

The nuclear problem remains huge. People are very disturbed and unsure about what is happening. "We do not usually discuss politics," said one adult student, "so we do not express our frustrations. In WW II we Japanese believed all the government told us and did not question what was said or what was not said. We blindly followed. I am very disappointed that we learned nothing from that and are repeating the same mistakes."

But Prime Minster Kan is being challenged. And people are watching carefully and beginning to express concern. Not by throwing stones, smashing windows, burning cars, carrying signs or demonstrating. But a deep underlying sense of mistrust of the government is very prevalent, even as people work together to pull their lives together.

Recently an artist friend of mine took his students to Minami-sanriku-cho. This is what he said about the experience. "I have been busy with the voluntary activity in Minami-sanriku-cho in which my students have been painting images on the newly-rebuilt fishermen's warehouse in. I feel better with the project." And another friend and translator wrote this:

"I went to Minami-sanriku on Wednesday with a couple from Perugia, Italy and their friend. They kindly donated two machines called skywater which can produce water from vapour in the air to Minami-sanriku.

http://www.skywater.it/english/home_en.html

"They placed one machine at an elementary school called Isakimae Elementary School in Utatsu area. The school used to be used as a place for dead bodies after Tsunami.

"The other machine was placed at Hotel Kanyo which has been used as a shelter since 11th March. 500 people used to live there, but now only 100 live there. But during day time still 500 people spend their time at the hotel as the place can get water and food.

"To my great surprise, Minami-sanriku area still does not have water supply! The area looks like war fields with only dusty roads, and piles of garbage, broken buildings.

"On 19th, I am going to go to Higashi Matsuhima with students from FSU to attend Cooking Activity for people in shelters."

Many friends want to come visit my new home. My old shack was very famous and no one can believe I am in a more stable modern place. So they want to check it out with their own eyes. Last week some friends came and we talked a lot about what is happening in this area and to Japan as a whole. "Life simply is not the same," one woman said. "There is always a nagging feeling that so much more work needs to be done, that people are still unsettled and suffering, that another major quake and tsunami could come anytime. After all, we just had three very strong quakes in two days! We talk about trying to get our lives back to normal. But what is normal? No one really knows any more."

. . .

But even so, there are some very healthy things happening. One of the best, I feel, is a huge festival in the making. Usually August is a time of regional merry-making here in Tohoku. There are some very famous and well-attended festivals in this region then. But this year tourism is practically dormant here. So, the local governments want to encourage people to come back and to enjoy the splendors of this area.

So, in mid-July there will be a once-in-a-lifetime assembly of the major summer festivals of all Tohoku. Akita will come bringing its tall shoulder lanterns and Kanto performers; Aomori will arrive with a magnificently painted Nebuta float; Yamagata will dance its famous Hanagasa with abundantly flowered hats; Iwate will bring Morioka's Sansa dance; poor, struggling Fukushima will offer its Waraji straw sandal parade; and Miyagi will strut its famous Susume Odori, the Sparrow Dance.

But before all that upcoming excitement, here in Sendai there has already been much activity of a joyous nature. The other day, for example, as I headed downtown, I was surprised to hear the excitement of a festival. Sendai's major events are usually held earlier (although not this year) or later, so I was curious. Suddenly I turned a corner and there were group after group of dancers and musicians, all dressed in their finest. They had on vivid happi jackets, red and gold headgear, closely fitting trousers, and faces painted with a long white line down the nose. Ah yes, sparrows doing the Susume Odori.

Each group performed the same dance with fans flipping like sparrows' tails, heads jerking like teeny birds pecking for food, legs bent and feet tapping just as a sparrow's would. There were drummers and cymbals, flutes and banners, shouts and chanting, "Sau-ray, Sau-ray, Sau-ray, Sau-ray."

All were forceful and proud, rhythmically expressing the power of the indomitable Japanese spirit. "We shall never be overwhelmed. We shall overcome these challenging times. We will come out of this stronger and better. We as a people have stretched from time beyond time and will continue long after we as individuals are forgotten."

It felt as if everyone were there: old and young, tall and short, pretty and plain, working people, students, housewives, and children. Everyone was included. Everyone was welcomed. And everyone wanted to be there, to be part of the incredible energy of reassurance and resurgence.

There were so many beautiful images that stood out. Men with rock-hard, rippling muscles, women with bright eyes and ruby-red lips, and children dolled up in glittering finery. Little folk as young as five were often in the very front, leading their four-generation band of Sparrow Dancers and musicians. One group included a very gentle, mentally challenged man who drooled, but banged a drum in perfect cyclical rhythm. Another group had babies in carriages. They might not have been able to walk yet, but the beat and the rhythm of the chanting and dancing were being embedded into the very framework of their being. To be sure, they, too, will be carriers of this ancient unifying tradition.

My favorite by far was a teeny girl of about three. She was with her attentive grandmother, watching the parade going by. Suddenly she spotted her mother, one of the dancers. She burst out of her gran's embrace and flew to her mother, who had crouched down to receive her with welcoming arms. The mother, beaming and still dancing, picked up her little princess, and swung her onto her back, while never missing a beat. Then the two of them blended back into the cluster of dancers, swaying and chanting their way down the street and out of sight.

Group after colorful group performed that day. Some were big and raucous, others were small and dignified. Some had mostly women and girls, others predominately men and boys, while some were a perfect balance of the two. But whatever the assemblage, the spirit was one of total oneness, of reassurance, and of strength to "fight" – for survival and for a rebirth into something new, not only for us, but also for many generations to come.

Those two days of chanting and dancing from morning to night were all in preparation for the big festival to come. Hopefully then hordes from all over Japan will congregate to encourage and support us with glorious shouts of "We are. We are great. We will not give up. We can do anything if we work together!"

"Sau-ray, Sau-ray, Sau-ray, Sau-ray."

Love,

Anne

LETTER TWENTY-SEVEN

July 1, 2011

Dear Family and Friends,

Although my main job is in a university, I also teach privately. My favorite of those lessons is an advanced English class for adults. I have been teaching them for many years, so we have become good friends. Since they are well educated and talkative, I always try to introduce topics that will enable them to think deeply and to express themselves freely.

Recently I found the following story by Pema Chödrön in a lovely magazine called *Sacred Journey*. It is a clear, seemingly simple tale about life as seen from a Buddhist perspective. I added questions and comments (please note the indented italics), which the students were to discuss one by one as they worked their way through the story. I was curious to hear their thoughts because this piece was written by an American Buddhist for a western audience. And sure enough, I learned a lot from my class the day we studied this tale.

Dusk on the River by Pema Chödrön (see next page) is offered first in its original, uninterrupted form – then once again, accompanied by Anne's questions and comments for her students.

Dusk on the River

From the book, *Start Where You Are* – by Pema Chödrön

A man is enjoying himself on a river at dusk.

He is in a small boat. And suddenly he sees another boat coming down the river towards him.

It seems so nice that someone else is enjoying the river on a nice summer evening.

Then he suddenly realizes the boat is coming towards him faster and faster.

He begins to get upset and shouts, "Hey, hey! Watch out! For heaven's sake, turn aside. Don't hit me!"

But the boat just comes faster and faster, right towards him. By this time he is standing in the boat, screaming and shaking his fists.

Then the boat smashes right into him.

He sees that it is an empty boat.

This is the classic story of our whole life situation.

Dusk on the River

From the book, *Start Where You Are* – by Pema Chödrön

(Anne's questions and comments to her class are in italics):

A man is enjoying himself on a river at dusk.

What do you imagine he is thinking?

He is in a small boat. And suddenly he sees another boat coming down the river towards him.

What image do you have of this scene?
Describe the boats and the people in them.

It seems so nice that someone else is enjoying the river on a nice summer evening.

Do you get pleasure knowing others are enjoying themselves at the same time you are? Give examples.

Then he suddenly realizes the boat is coming towards him faster and faster.

Why do you think this is happening?

He begins to get upset and shouts, "Hey, hey! Watch out! For heaven's sake, turn aside. Don't hit me!

What do you think will happen next?

But the boat just comes faster and faster, right towards him. By this time he is standing in the boat, screaming and shaking his fists.

What do you think he will do next?

Then the boat smashes right into him.

How do you imagine the man is feeling?
What do you think he says?

He sees that it is an empty boat.

How do you imagine the man is feeling now?
And what is he thinking?

This is the classic story of our whole life situation.

Why does the story end with this statement?
What does this mean?
Do you agree with it?
Please give examples.

My students became very involved in this story, discussing each question from many different angles. Here are a few things they said.

First, they all agreed that as Japanese and Buddhists they would not have become angry that the other boat was coming towards them rapidly. They also said they would not have stood in the boat, screaming and shaking their fists. "We Japanese don't do that sort of thing," they reassured me. "We are taught not to express our anger openly. Rather we try to discuss things until we can reach an agreement in which everyone's point of view is taken into consideration."

Another student made this comment: "Everyone has good and bad in them. That is natural. So when someone becomes angry, we wait. We are sure that a more positive side will soon come to the fore. We prefer to look upon the good side of others, if we can. And if we cannot, it is better just to walk away."

"In my case," said one man, "I would immediately have steered out of the way of the boat racing towards me. Why should I get angry at him, blame him, or expect him to move for me?"

One woman then added, "I would have apologized immediately (to the empty boat, or maybe to her own!), but that is not what a westerner would do, I don't think. When we get international drivers' licenses, we are instructed never to say we are sorry if we have an accident. But here in Japan, we always apologize, even if we are not wrong. We say we are sorry for many reasons. The most important is that we want to be polite. Saying we are sorry shows our respect for the other person and we consider saying 'Gomen nasai' (I am sorry) to be very polite. Another reason we say we are sorry, even is someone hit us, is because maybe we were in the other person's way. Or possibly it is because we are sorry to have brought disharmony into the world. Maybe, too, it is because we know that this situation will cause problems for the person in the future. There are so many reasons why we apologize here in Japan. And it most often does not have anything to do with being right or wrong."

...

And sure enough a few days after this class a former student sent me an e-mail in which she told me she was getting a divorce. But then she continued by saying, "I must apologize to you about this. You came to my wedding, but now I am divorcing. I feel so bad for doing this to you. I am sorry." Her comment came as a surprise to me. But then I remembered the strong sense of duty that Japanese feel towards others, often in dimensions that people from other cultures might not even be aware of.

"For me, I see this story as the recent tragic events in this area. The earthquake and tsunami came to us without warning. And then the nuclear problems began and continue. Of course, we are not happy with the nuclear situation or the government's handling of it. We hope that something will soon be done about those human errors. But we do not go out and shake our fists to show extreme anger. We also did not scream and yell at the awful happenings of nature. Personally the more I think about it, the more I believe the basic psychic structure of the Japanese comes because throughout history we have experienced one huge tragedy after another. We had the enormous Jogan Earthquake in 869 AD. There are mass graves that tell us that thousands of people died then, too. Then in 1611 there was the Keicho Sanriku Earthquake. And in 1671 the Enpo Boso Offshore Quake hit. Also in 1923 there was a tremendous quake and fire in the Tokyo area in which over 100,000 people died. And the recent quake in Kobe caused a lot of deaths, too. We Japanese live on the edge of risk always. And I believe that is why we have learned to accept what comes to us – "Shoga nai (It can't be helped) without getting angry or blaming others."

...

"We also have balance," added another. "We know about the reality of earthquakes and tsunami and the possibility of losing everything very suddenly. But that is not the full picture. We also have a saying that goes like this: 'When there is an earthquake, go into the bamboo forest.' Bamboo has long roots, so a bamboo forest is more stable than other areas. And in everyday life, if there is upset or anger, we can always retreat to areas, even inside ourselves, that are stable and secure. Then we wait until the high emotion is past before we try to deal with it."

...

Another student saw this story from a different angle. "The boat was empty. I think we live always knowing that life itself is empty. Today we may have things; tomorrow we might not. Even our own life, we have it now, but we know it is passing through us. That is basic to our way of thinking and to how we live each day. That helps us to be acutely aware, and hopefully appreciative of this very moment, now."

One final comment seemed to sum up a lot. "This story was definitely written by and for westerners. We Japanese somehow live knowing we are part of nature and of one another. And that is true even when nature shows her very destructive side. If you think of the tsunami as unleashed anger, then recent past events have shown us how terrible raging anger can be. That should be a good reminder of why we do not express fury in destructive ways. Also we are not separate and isolated from nature or from others. And we know that we have to work together to survive. I hear that there are people in America who live all by themselves far out in the woods. How do they do that? I can't imagine it! For us we believe that being part of each other is fundamental to being human. Don't you think so, too?"

Even though I have lived immersed in this culture for many years, I realize how my own psychic structure and thought patterns still remain very western. So I always appreciate a class like this one. And I am grateful, too, to be nudged yet again towards other ways of being in the world.

Love,

Anne

LETTER TWENTY-EIGHT

July 14, 2011

Dear Family and Friends,

Even though the initial intensity of the March 11 disaster may have subsided, many people still feel a deep tugging to help Japanese disaster victims. Since that subtle pull is strong and persistent, people are finding very creative ways to bring hope and healing to this part of the world.

Three efforts in particular have found their way to me. The first is an offer by a caring individual and his family. The second is an Australian concern called *Wishes on Wings*. And the third is an American project named *500 Frogs*.

Here is the first, a beautiful offer given by a very sensitive, loving family.

"Years ago we spent some time in Sendai, and the coastal villages to the north, as I work as a marine biologist. Our team had tracked a sea turtle from Baja California, Mexico to Sendai (7,000 miles in 368 days), the first animal ever tracked swimming across an ocean.

"While in Sendai, we experienced such wonderful hospitality and kindness from strangers. In our work we walked a long stretch of coast to the north of Sendai until we reached Adelita's (the turtle) final location. All along the way we were greeted and taken care of.

"Our family and my work has been connected to Sendai ever since.

"Our daughters, Grayce (9) and Julia (6), were thinking about how they could help people in Sendai and decided that they'd like to offer their room to a girl from Sendai who may want to take a break in the redwoods of California...sort of a reverse sea turtle migration.

"They'd like to host a Japanese family to come stay with us, to help a girl their age to feel less stress. They remember what it was like when our home was nearly lost to a massive forest fire."

. . .

Truly, this first offer manifests the beauty of empathy and compassion at work, individual to individual.

. . .

The second of these efforts, *Wishes on Wings,* began almost immediately after the Great East Japan Earthquake and resulting tsunami obliterated most of the Pacific coastline settlements of this area. This organization has two main projects. One is on an emotional and spiritual level, the other very practical. The first was addressed by volunteers who made thousands of origami cranes, uniting them into long garlands called Senbazuru. For centuries these winged messengers have been symbols of hope and good wishes for those in difficulty. The other level on which work of *Wishes on Wings* was very down to earth. They did fundraising, not to give cash donations, but rather to offer very practical items, such as a kitchen in a community center, or equipment for a daycare center and a school. The Senbazuru and fund raising activities are drawing to a close. So the next part is to find the best place for the equipment they wish to offer. To get a clearer idea of the work, here are the exact words of Cate Juno, one of the main organizers of this project.

"Actually, *Wishes on Wings* has been set up specifically to rally support for the survivors of the Japan disaster. We are doing this in two ways:

"Firstly, we are encouraging people to send messages of hope which we are writing onto origami paper and making them into paper cranes to create a senbazuru (or many senbazuru we hope!) We are doing this so that people feel they are making an emotional connection with those who are suffering, and so that the people who receive these messages know that the world at large has not forgotten them. We think this is an important aspect of 'giving'.

"Secondly, we are collecting monetary donations with the aim of contributing to a specific project in the disaster area once the task of rebuilding begins. We would {like} to find a specific project such as cooking equipment for a community centre, or play equipment for a daycare centre, or equipment for a school, etc.

"This project is also going into our local schools so that children can feel that they can help, too. We are in Western Australia but have a friend in Atlanta who is also starting this project there. We are also gathering financial support from other small groups here who are collecting donations and want to work together to create a single project.

"One of our team members is a university student from Sendai who has decided to stay and continue his studies because his parents have said this is the best way he can contribute to the future of Sendai. But it is very difficult for Koki to focus on his studies and so this project is helping him to cope with his personal tragedy.

"We have put up a Website: www.wishesonwings.com – and a Facebook page, *Wishes on Wings*.

. . .

Last week I met Koki, who had returned to this area for a few weeks. It was the first time he had come home since the disaster. When I met him, he was in total shock and very conflicted as to what his next move should be. "Should I continue my studies in Perth?" he queried. "Or should I come back here to help? I really, really want to be here now. What in all of this have I really experienced? I feel so left out, as if I should have been here during the earthquake and tsunami. But what can I do now?"

We talked for a long time, but his deep existential questioning has just begun. Hopefully it will lead him to unfold into a sense of what he is meant to do for those who have and still are suffering tremendously.

. . .

The third endeavor that has become part of my life is *500 Frogs*. One of the persons involved, Nanci Caron, is an occupational therapist in California. She contacted me through odemagazine.com to ask if I would like to become involved in *500 Frogs*. Nanci was fascinated by the philosophy behind these teeny creatures of hope. "Kaeru" means two things in Japanese. One is "frog" and the other is "to return home". In addition, frogs carry very rich and deep symbolism in Japanese culture. So images of these wonderful beings seemed an appropriate item to give to children who had suffered great loss during the March 11 trauma and beyond.

Her exact words are better than mine, so here they are:

"Meanwhile, I am busy with the project with my patients, and some of my personal friends. People want to be part of a bigger, creative effort to send a message of hope and caring to the Japanese children. Some of my biggest, toughest, and most 'complicated' patients are willing participants in the project ... it provides them an outlet for their spirit of compassion and desire to do something positive for someone. I think having children in mind is the biggest motivator. My patients relate to the feeling of being displaced (because they live in a residential psychiatric hospital), and to the conditions of loneliness and loss. To illustrate the personal touch some of the frogs get, here is one painted by one of my patients - a former tattoo artist. I can imagine this one going to an older child or teenager..."

...

And the founder of this amazing project, Deb Buckler, has a lot more to add.

"When the earthquake hit Japan, I was heartbroken for those people who had lost so much. And continue to suffer. The economy here is bad, and few people can give money to help out. Sure, you can donate to the Red Cross, or send a few dollars here or there, but I wanted to do something personal. My husband, Randy, and I run a home based resin casting business here on the central coast, and we have a little resin frog that Randy made for fundraising. As it turned out, we happened to have 100 of our little frogs in inventory here, so I went to my groups and asked if folks would like to help paint them so we could send them to the children of Japan. I felt a personally hand painted frog, made in America, would be a nice token of our love and concern for them. Something physical they can put in their pocket and carry around. Possibly their only 'hand made in America' item that they owned.

"Well ... within moments after I asked for help with the frogs, all 100 were reserved. By the next day, another 400 were reserved, and we are now up to 600 frogs being individually hand painted by folks literally all over the world. Children, adults, groups, families are involved. Because of our connections to these artists, Switzerland and Australia are no further away then my keyboard. So! I am sending frogs to Sweden, Germany, wherever, they paint them, sign them and return them to me. It's QUITE a process!!

"When I started *500 Frogs,* my focus was totally the children of Japan. And that continues to be the case. However, as this project evolves, I realize there is more healing going on in a peripheral sense. As the person holding this frog pours their love and compassion into it, they are receiving a blessing that will enhance their life forever. I have received some pretty amazing letters already. Nanci's experience with her patients is a good example. But the biggest thrill was when a small, very poor school in Fresno, California painted 30 frogs for the children. These are middle school kids ... 12 to 16 years old, underprivileged and disadvantaged ... so poor, their teacher had to buy the frogs for them and we absorbed the shipping. These kids have nothing, and have always been on the receiving end of society. But now, for once, they were able to give something to someone who had even less then THEY did. They painted their hearts out on the frogs and most of them wrote such tender, loving letters to the children, they will bring tears when you read them. These kids are so proud of doing this, they are now looking for other "random acts of kindness" they can do!

"It is my hope, that the children who get these frogs will keep them forever, and will remember that someone, in another country, cared very much about them during their desperate time. Perhaps it will affect that child's decisions toward the rest of the world when he is an adult."

. . .

Happily a Japanese friend helped to locate a perfect place for these "hoppers".

On August 20 there will be a children's festival in Higashi Matsushima, a very badly hit area. The organizer of that event is thrilled with these gifts, coming from so far away and filled with so much love. So, that is where they shall find their homes, in the hearts of the children who receive them.

If you would like more information on this truly remarkable project, please go to http://500frogs.com/

You might also enjoy the following article about it, at:

http://www.sanluisobispo.com/2011/07/24/1694538/japan earthquake-atascadero-frogs.html#storylink=omni_popular

Love,

Anne

LETTER TWENTY-NINE

July 16, 2011

Dear Family and Friends,

Northeast Japan, Tohoku, has six prefectures. Although not all of them were directly affected by the Great East Japan Earthquake, as it is now officially labeled, each one feels a duty – and a strong desire – to band together in support of one another. And indeed we are all in this together. The entire area is suffering economically from the recent disaster. The fishing industry was all but wiped out (but is painstakingly struggling to revive); many small factories that make parts for cars and machinery were also obliterated; beaches and coastal farms were inundated by black, oily, salty tsunami waters, while others were contaminated by nuclear radiation. Considering the confusion and ongoing problems here, people who might normally come for their summer vacation in Tohoku, are avoiding this region completely. So, tourism, which accounts for a huge percent of the economy up here, is almost at a standstill. Along with those dire realities, the rainy season ended three weeks early, causing temperatures to soar as much as 10° C above normal and bringing great concerns for the rice, which needs ample water to grow.

But precisely because of these seemingly unending headaches, the authorities of this region decided to put on a once-in-a-lifetime event. Each prefecture would send its main summer festival's dancers and performers to Sendai for two days of festivities. There would also be various other activities going on throughout the day. One of those, for example, was a tent where children could draw pictures. Another was an exhibition of Manga art related to the "gambaru" spirit we all need. There was also an area offering free

146

foot soaks in thermal waters. But the most unusual were tubs full of teeny fish into which people put their legs or arms. The fish gently tickled the person's extremities as they ate unhealthy microbes on the skin. People said they came out of those cleansing tubs fully refreshed and invigorated.

The events were scheduled from morning to evening on both days. But because of the oppressive heat, I decided to go in the early morning, glean what I could, go home for a shower and nap, and then return later when a big parade was to be held.

The morning was rather pleasant with things happening in small booths dotted around the main event square and park. Intuitively I wandered over to the City Hall and found myself face to face with Iwate Prefecture's Sansa dancers. They had on big hats shaped like bright red lotus flowers, traditional summer "kimonos,", called "yukatas", and colorful sashes. They danced and swayed to the beat of drums and seemed to really enjoy themselves. Interestingly, and to my delight, men and women all wore the exact same costume and danced the exact same steps, while a few played the exact same rhythm on their drums. I had never seen the gender equality expressed to such an extent of sameness as in that particular dance. And I found it curious and very refreshing.

Another flowered hat performance came from Yamagata Prefecture and was called "Hanagasa", Flower Hat. Here, too, men and women dressed up similarly, this time in straw hats pulled down over their ears and covered in brightly colored, shimmering flowers. Men and women both danced, more like a hop, as men directed them with drums. Possibly the hopping was an imitation of grasshoppers since all of these summer festivals are related to farming in one way or another.

Fukushima Prefecture sent an enormous "Waraji", which is a woven sandal made from rice stalks. This "Waraji" was a very long, beautifully crafted, almost boat-like, specimen of traditional footwear. It sat majestically in one quiet corner of the festival arena, waiting patiently for the evening parade.

Aomori Prefecture sent a huge float with paper maché figures, called "Nebuta". The scene depicted was of a long ago battle victory. It had fierce warrior faces and screaming horses arching upwards. At night it was lit from within and supported by many men in "happi" festival jackets and with "tenugui" cloths wrapped around their shaved heads.

Miyagi Prefecture had deer dancers with performers in elaborately dyed costumes and a veil over their faces. They had long antlers made of many flowerets of white paper. They magnificently bobbed down the street in perfect prancing rhythm as they beat their individual drums.

The most energetic performance, the "Kanto", was from Akita Prefecture. This festival is famous for its huge 12-meter high poles with many horizontal bars that taper at the top. Each bar has a row of illuminated paper lanterns. The entire structure represents rice stalks heavy with grain. The "Kanto" performance is done only by men. They wear dark blue "happi" jackets and white shorts. Most sit in a circle clapping a special rhythmic beat, while a few men hoist one of those heavy, illuminated "rice stalks" onto their shoulders, hips, hands, or foreheads. They stagger to the beat of the clapping, all the while balancing the swaying "Kanto" poles on one part of their bodies and then another. Suddenly another man will leap up, slip into the place of his friend, and continue the stomping, rhythmic balancing act. That afternoon the expression of manly prowess went on and on, and was captivating, invigorating, and truly a pleasure to behold.

The evening was far more crowded than the morning. In fact, almost every local seemed to be there, plus bus loads of people who had come from far away. Just like the tsunami that was much, much larger than anyone had ever expected, the hordes of people were far more numerous than anyone ever imagined. They soon filled up all the sidewalks, the island between the street lanes, the parks, then the nearby shops, and finally the road itself where the parade was to be held. And even then more people kept coming.

The police had loud speakers and issued commands in a beautifully Japanese way: "Would everyone please be so kind as to move back so the performers can get by?" Or "We hate to bother you, but would you all mind making a pathway for people to get through?" Or "We would appreciate your thoughtful consideration to move back a bit."

But people were too jammed together to budge. It was beastly hot and everyone was sweating and feeling tired. But even so, most people smiled, even laughed, as they tried to keep their balance or avoid getting stepped on. However, a few fights did break out, but each time someone immediately got between the two angry men and said, "Here! Here! Let's not have any of that, especially now!" And the two would back off, still glaring at each other, and then squeeze their way in opposite directions, hopefully to get a much-needed beer.

The street was so jammed that the parade was unable to move. So the performers ended up doing the best they could staying in one place.

It took forever, but somehow I moved with the pushing waves of humanity, and eked my way out of the densest part of the crowd and onto a small street, still thronged with people, but with more breathing space. I wound my way through side streets and eventually swung back round towards my trusty bicycle. During that time I was able to pop a few photos of adorable kids on their fathers' shoulders, young girls in festive pink "yukatas", little boys being silly, mothers trying to keep a semblance of order, couples sharing ice cream cones, and old people holding hands. The entire experience that evening was a disappointment as far as watching the performances went, but a huge success in witnessing the diversity of people joining together with a common thread of hope for a better future for us all.

Love,

Anne

LETTER THIRTY

July 19, 2011

Dear Family and Friends,

Izumi's mother, Suenaga San, is very short. She only comes up to my waist, but she is not a midget. Many people here her age, 88, are tiny. That is because they were born before World War II, after which the Americans introduced milk and meat into the Japanese diet.

I call Izumi's mom "Okaasan", which means "Mother". That is a polite and loving way of addressing a woman who is kind to you, as she has been to me. Okaasan was born in 1923 at the exact time that the devastating Kanto Earthquake took place, causing a raging fire that killed hundreds of thousands and destroyed much of Tokyo. That quake struck just at noon, when people were preparing lunch using gas or wood. Buildings at that time were very close together and made of timber, so when the earth shook violently, tossing everything hither and yon, it also caused stoves to overturn, and entire homes to be consumed by fire. "I came into the world at a dramatic and tragic moment," Okaasan said, "And I have seen a lot in my 88 years."

Here in Japan age 88 is special. The characters for that number can be rearranged in a pretty design that means "rice". So the 88th birthday is called "Beiju", or "The Age of Rice". And since that important grain is the basis of life here, and since until recently very few people made it to the honorable age of 88, "Beiju" was, and still is, a time of great celebration and rejoicing.

Okaasan was the oldest of eight children. She was able to finish high school, but started work immediately after in order to help her parents financially. "I was not the kind who stayed in one company. I moved about. But I always worked in printing firms. I did not make much, but that was normal for women back then. And my parents were grateful for whatever I brought home. They took every yen I earned. I was not allowed to keep any of it for myself. Of course, I lived at home with my parents and siblings. That, too, was normal and expected at that time. It was during the war, too, so everyone was hungry and needed money. We were lucky to have relatives with farms, so we could eat, but barely enough.

"I remember when Sendai was bombed. It was terrible. The planes came over and suddenly there was fire and smoke everywhere. People were screaming and running to find shelter. So many died. It was really, really terrifying. But when the war ended, American soldiers came. At first we were really afraid of them, but they were nice to us. They let us come up close to stare at them and gave us candy. And it was such a relief to have the war over. And we got food again. That included meat and milk, which we never really had before."

Okaasan was lucky to have work at that time. And as she moved from job to job, always looking for more pay, she landed in one company where she met a handsome man. He was two years younger than she, but that did not matter to them, so before long they were married. "He was wonderful. Very gentle, very kind. He was the only son in a family of many girls, so he knew what a woman was and always treated me well. He earned less than I did, though, but we arranged things so that we used my money to live on and saved his. That way we could buy land."

Their lot was on a forested hill on the outskirts of Sendai. Every weekend she and her spouse would go there to clear the land. "We did it all ourselves. I got to be really good with an ax," she told me with pride. "And before long we had enough land cleared so we could build a house. Of course, we stacked all the trees we had cut and used that wood for cooking and for heating the bath. It was such a wonderful time then. We had a dream and were working hard to make it come true."

When I told Izumi the stories Okaasan was telling me, she got very excited and said, "Oh, I remember that house! It was in a forested area and the bath was separate. I remember stepping over stones to get to it and then sinking myself into the hot water, looking out over the trees and sky, hearing bird calls, breathing in the fresh air. It was so nice!"

Okaasan told me with a shy laugh that she adored dancing. "My husband and I would go out several times a month. I loved dressing up, putting on make-up, and heading out for an evening of fun. And downtown Sendai was so exciting then. The shops were friendly and Saturday night was so lively. I can still picture those times even today." She would then get up and swing her hips a bit to show me what a delight those times had been.

"My husband really wanted a child, so we tried and tried, but I just could not keep one in my body. But finally I conceived and Izumi was born when I was 40. Nowadays many women are having their children late in life, but in those times it was very unusual. Of course, we were elated to have her. She and her father adored each other and spent many happy hours together."

Izumi herself told me her earliest memory was holding onto her father's shoulders when he carried her strapped on his back. "I remember my love for him and the safety I felt being so close to him," she reminisced. But very sadly he died of cancer when Izumi was in her early 20s. So from then on Izumi has been responsible for her mother.

With Izumi's pay checks she and her mother decided to build a new home on their property. There were many other houses surrounding them by that time, but they had a wall to support their house on the hill and to allow others to build below them. That wall was made of huge, solid stones that seemed strong enough to last forever. However, in the Great East Japan Earthquake of March 11, the shaking was so great that the wall literally came tumbling down. The boulders bounced down the hill, smacking into Izumi's uncle's home below and just missing the homes of the other neighbors. Since then life has been stressful like never before.

Since the earthquake Izumi and Okaasan are in a "doughnut hole" financially. People are getting some compensation from the government for damage to their property during the disaster. But Izumi's mother refuses to leave her home and enter an evacuation shelter, even though the house is sitting precariously on the edge of a cliff. "I am 88. This is my home. I want to die here. And if I go tomorrow, that is fine. I have lived a full life. I am not budging," she says stubbornly. That means that Izumi cannot get government compensation money. And she does not earn enough to repair the wall as well as make house payments. So for months she has been trying to work out a way to deal with this. She has gone to many banks for loans. She has talked to several repair companies. She has calculated what all this will cost and how many years it will take to pay back the loan. She has also had to deal with the nervous neighbors. Thank heavens suing does not happen here often, but even so, the people below her are not too pleased. They all had a meeting to discuss boundaries and wall repairs the other day. Izumi was terrified to face them all at once, but later told me they all just wanted the wall fixed and "Shoganai" when it came to borders between the houses. So Izumi continues to be straddled between her mother, the neighbors, and the unaffordable expense of repairs.

Trying to persuade her mother to move does not seem an option. Filial piety runs strong in Asia.

To make matters worse, her uncle in the house below went out to inspect the fallen wall after a particularly heavy rain. He slipped and fell, breaking three bones, one of them in his neck. The neighbor who had been making the greatest fuss about the wall issue saw him and immediately called Okaasan. Izumi later told me that that bit of kindness, despite the feud going on between them, really meant a great deal to her. "Now I see we still have a good connection on important levels. And that helps me a lot," she said to me. Her uncle is now in the ICU of a local hospital and after work Izumi goes to check on him and deal with paper work.

No one knows where all this will lead. We go one day at a time. I say "we" because after the quake Izumi and Okaasan were very, very kind and let me stay with them for five weeks after my own house became uninhabitable. "We are family," they say to me. "So you can stay as long as you need or want." But I did move on, thanks to their connections. Getting a place to live here is extremely difficult now with so many displaced persons about. But their magic brought me the good fortune of an apartment. With all their kindness to me, I feel a great obligation towards them. So with the wall business, too, I feel a great desire to help. How? By love and support, of course, but hopefully in more concrete ways, too, as my own circumstances allow.

Izumi and Okaasan are not alone in being in financial difficulties now. Many, many people cannot afford to repair their property and have not received enough or any money from the government. I spoke to one student the other day. She told me her home had been inundated by the tsunami on the first floor, but not too damaged. So after a few days of evacuation, they returned and cleaned up the place. Even though their neighbors' houses collapsed, there is an upturned truck in their yard, and the stench and enormous flies are almost unbearable, they are living in their home. "We have no choice. We don't have money to move," she explained to me. Unbelievably they have water, electricity and gas. The unevenness of damage and repair everywhere (some places totally damaged right next to ones fully in tact, for example, or houses half demolished, but with laundry hanging outside) is something very difficult for the mind and heart to wrap themselves around into an acceptable cohesiveness. Life is not a tidy either-or these days. It is a blending of all possibilities happening simultaneously and contingently. For my Western psyche this is causing an upheaval in my entire worldview. But the Japanese seem to take it in their stride, saying, "That is how life is. And so 'Shoganai'."

Love,

Anne

The Responses

Response One

March 15, 2011

Thank you very much for your concern with us.

I've just regained the Internet connection. Your e-mail is so much encouraging. Lucky my family and I are OK; however I have been trying to find out the situations of some students and friends whom I lost contact with since the earthquake and tsunami attacked this area.

There are still many students staying and living on campus. Some lost their houses and the others are not sure if their families are OK. When I met them, I just couldn't find right word to cheer them up.

Today was supposed to be a graduation day which was postponed and might be canceled. When I saw the students at the campus housing this morning, they served me a special breakfast that the juniors cooked for the seniors to celebrate the day. The meal was cold, but really special. I won't forget the taste of it. I am convinced that my students will overcome this tragedy with the positive attitude. I intend to emulate them.

Thanks again for your attention.

Nori

Norihiko Seto
Sendai, Japan

RESPONSE TWO

March 18, 2011

Anne - beautifully said and so heartfelt.

I am in tears reading it, not for fears for your safety, but for your wonderful courage and capacity to live through this time in history from the perspective that you have just expressed.

It is certainly a powerful lesson for ego and for your own spiritual journey and I wish you absolute love, peace and compassion as you go through it.

As you say you are amongst dear friends there who have also been through some of the darkest days of their lives right now, so for you I suspect it probably is the right place to be, amongst souls who can empathise with each other.

Whatever happens, you know you also have many friends and family around the globe who dearly love you and are thinking of you.

Wishing you much courage and beams of light to illuminate the darkness and thank you so much for including me in your incredible messages.

Oceans of love,

Lynne xxxxx

Lynne Dorning Sands
on board ship SV Amarula, South Africa

RESPONSE THREE

March 19, 2011

Hi Anne + enormous ego :D

Although from a selfish perspective I would love for you to be safe and sound, thousands of miles from earthquakes and potential nuclear fallout I couldn't for the life of me see you, in my mind's eye, making the decision to do that. Obviously people can do uncharacteristic things in times of panic – hence my asking the question in my last e-mail – but the way you've been describing your life over the past week: the joy at finding food, an open real estate agency, at having down blankets and an electric fire, it never sounded like you were going to get up and leave. You, your friend and her mother are sharing the load and achieving things none of you could on your own and you are very much part of what's happening there, in the best way possible. I hope that together you'll be found another place to rent, and that your friend's mother's farmer friend will be able to keep you in rice, and that the little family market will keep up with the demand for fresh supplies. Obviously that's among my other, many, unspoken and larger hopes.

Something else you're doing by staying here is communicating what's actually happening to us all so far away, and I think that has enormous value. It's really easy to lose sight of the day-to-day struggle people are facing, when the news tends to concentrate on the big ticket stories. I also think your decision to stay is a humbling lesson in assessing life's priorities to us lucky people, especially here in Altinkum where people love a good moan about the roads, the noisy dogs and the price of beer.

So, basically, by choosing to stay, you've confirmed you really are the person I see you as: brave, caring, generous, wise. I don't want you to martyr yourself for the sake of my vision of you, but instead please make the most of it because I think the whole thing about Japan is that together you can all make a difference.

One more thing... silly, I know, but I am a little worried about losing touch... have you thought about setting up a webmail account of some kind so you have another option, if you need it, to going into your shack to answer your e-mails? Every time I see an e-mail from you in my mailbox it's confirmation that you're still okay and if your house falls down, or you find somewhere to stay that's too far away to go back and forth then I'll miss that...

Oh, and one MORE last thing – I asked before if there was anything I could do, and I did mean that in a practical sense... is there anything we can do, from far away, to make life easier? Is there a particular organisation that you see helping people out that might benefit from donations or something? Obviously there are the big international ones but I'm presuming that the more removed they are from the actual people dishing up the soup, the more diluted a donation of any kind is.

So that's it for now from me but - in your words - OCEANS of love.

xxxxxxx

Laura, Hakan & Hulya

Laura Çetinkaya
Altinkum, Turkey

RESPONSE FOUR

March 19, 2011

Dearest Anne,

It has never crossed my mind that you would leave... one doesn't leave one's people in time of need. I remember stories of my grandparents living through WWI and WWII and my parents being only 9 years old when the WWII started, what hardships they have lived through yet all that made them more beautiful with that inner beauty that come only from a knowing spirit that went through fire... and it is exactly what you're reporting.

I think your stories are so poignant and I feel should be published in some magazine to show the world a more intimate and such beautiful picture of people living through this immense tragedy and somewhat balance that massive nuclear hysteria and fear in general that is being broadcast to us daily and spreading worldwide so quickly, serving perhaps a few interest groups but not people in Japan now.

Love – Ada

Ada Rotkiewicz
Polish-American
Allen, Texas USA

RESPONSE FIVE

March 19, 2011

Anne san,

You are sooooo brave.

And I am pleased that you decided to stay where you are and help people. Wow, not many people can do!

Right now, everyone around me is trying to help us staying here in NZ.

http://www.nzherald.co.nz/japantsunami/news/article.cfm?c_id=1503051&objectid=10713483

You know... I want to help you too, but there is nothing I can do. So, if you have chance, please go to my mother's place to get some food. My mother should be waiting for you to come.

Hope to see you soon!!

Love,

Mika

Mika Kato
Auckland, New Zealand

RESPONSE SIX

March 19, 2011

Anne - I'm speechless. You continue to amaze me. I can't say that I'm surprised of your decision though. As soon as I heard there was a bus out of Sendai for you, I knew that instant that you weren't going to go, despite encouragement from friends and family. You and the people of Japan are setting quite the example and your influence is spreading. Your letters have reached over 100,000 people now from Sydney to Europe to and across the US. I can't stop reading all the comments your words have generated. A sense of hope is spreading. As long as we pull together, all this will pass and we'll grow stronger from this. It's like you said, there is a sense of rebirthing going on and its a pleasure to watch the generosity and humility. Keep faith. With the path you've chosen, know that all hearts are pointing your way.

Here's a sampling of the responses you've gotten:

"Your words are incredibly inspiring."

"This letter in moving through the Net rapidly. Written by a woman teaching English in Japan. Inspiring. "

...

"Ann, thank you for being such a clear mirror of your place and your time. "

...

164

"This post... wow... You have to be full of humility to notice the good in others. It takes great faith in human goodness to do that. Instead of having faith in human goodness and being humble, so many of us we use a character flaw, Worry and allow it to expand into Fear. This lady - she's got the true humility thing going on! God bless those folks in Japan! "

. . .

"Yes Carol, it reflects just how caring and respectful the Japanese ppl are. My sister-in-law is from Okinawa and she is the MOST gentle person I have ever met. God only gives you what you can handle, not only as an individual, but as a country. Thanks for posting this. "

. . .

"Thanks and blessings from Sydney, Australia! Your blog got picked up by the Sydney Morning Herald (smh.com.au) and will reach millions of souls. Your open heart serves as a brilliant device which has the power to open the hearts of all of us readers. The behaviour in Sendai is evolutionary....KNOWING that our needs are met, we work together to manifest that Truth. May our collective open heart bring safety and health and community to every living soul in Japan, and the world. May our collective open heart bring peace and release to all souls perished in Japan, and the world. So much love to you! Namaste, Kimberella of Sydney"

. . .

"Dear Anne, Your message is being passed far beyond this blog. Now that I've found the source here I'll share it with more people.

You are touching many lives with your love filled words. THANK YOU for spreading the light. With Love for you and all your friends, Jan"

· · ·

"Your letter is penetrating lovely. I have tried to picture what it would be like to be in that reign as a survivor, and I pictured it precisely as you have described it; generosity, kindness, sacrifice, human-heartedness, and an almost involuntarily expanded view of life and the wonder of, well, everything. Thank you for confirming my expectations. "

· · ·

"Godspeed, Anne. For the past 7 days, my heart and mind is with Japan and its people. I can only offer my prayers that they may not lose hope and that they will overcome this unimaginable catastrophe. Through their resiliency, cooperation and unity I know that they will survive. Gambarimashou! "

"Very inspirational! The human SPIRIT is so beautiful."

· · ·

I am so impressed by the grace of these people.

Love and Light,

Katie

Katie Keenan

Former Editor of odemagazine.com (now odewire.com)
Portland, Oregon

RESPONSE SEVEN

March 20, 2011

Dear Anne,

I will have to stop reading your letters, they make me cry. Please continue to send them. We need to cry.

Love,

Sarah Sugiura

Chiba, Japan

RESPONSE EIGHT

March 23, 2011

Dear Anne,

Thank you so much for this valuable information.

Actually, *Wishes on Wings* has been set up specifically to rally support for the survivors of the Japan disaster. We are doing this in two ways:

Firstly, we are encouraging people to send messages of hope which we are writing onto origami paper and making them into paper cranes to create a senbazuru (or many senbazuru we hope!) We are doing this so that people feel they are making an emotional connection with those who are suffering, and so that the people who receive these messages know that the world at large has not forgotten them. We think this is an important aspect of 'giving.'

Secondly, we are collecting monetary donations with the aim of contributing to a specific project in the disaster area once the task of rebuilding begins. We would value your connections on the ground for helping to find a specific project such as cooking equipment for a community centre, or play equipment for a daycare centre, or equipment for a school, etc.

This project is also going into our local schools so that children can feel that they can help too. We are in Western Australia but have a friend in Atlanta who is also starting this project there. We are also gathering financial support from other small groups here who are collecting donations and want to work together to create a single project.

One of team members is a university student from Sendai who has decided to stay and continue his studies because his parents have said this is the best way he can contribute to the future of Sendai. But it is very difficult for Koki to focus on his studies and so this project is helping him to cope with his personal tragedy.

We have a website at: www. wishesonwings.com ... and a Facebook page: *Wishes on Wings*.

I hope you can stay in touch and continue to help us to find a suitable project in the near future.

Thank you again for your wonderful blog that keeps our hearts engaged,

Cate

Cate Feldman Perth,
Western Australia

RESPONSE NINE

March 25, 2011

Dear Anne,

Carl is sending me your daily reports. They're wonderful.

I've sent one or 2 on to friends, especially the one's who have been telling me to leave.

It's had a good effect on them!

Here is a poem that seems written for you.

Love and admiration,

Kristin

Kristin Newton
Tokyo, Japan

Subject: Fw: poem from the writer Miyazawa Kenji

A poem from the *(late)* writer, Miyazawa Kenji which you may appreciate at this point.

Ame Ni Mo Makezu *(Be not Defeated by the Rain)*
By Miyazawa Kenji (1896-1933)
Translation by David Sulz – followed by the original in Japanese

not losing to the rain
not losing to the wind
not losing to the snow nor to summer's heat
with a strong body
unfettered by desire
never losing temper
cultivating a quiet joy
every day four bowls of brown rice
miso and some vegetables to eat
in everything
count yourself last and put others before you
watching and listening, and understanding
and never forgetting
in the shade of the woods of the pines of the fields
being in a little thatched hut
if there is a sick child to the east
going and nursing over them
if there is a tired mother to the west
going and shouldering her sheaf of rice
if there is someone near death to the south
going and saying there's no need to be afraid
if there is a quarrel or a lawsuit to the north
telling them to leave off with such waste
when there's drought, shedding tears of sympathy
when the summer's cold, wandering upset
called a nobody by everyone
without being praised

without being blamed
such a person
I want to become

雨ニモマケズ

風ニモマケズ

雪ニモ夏ノ暑サニモマケヌ

丈夫ナカラダヲモチ

慾ハナク

決シテ瞋ラズ

イツモシヅカニワラッテイル

一日ニ玄米四合ト

味噌ト少シノ野菜ヲタベ

アラユルコトヲ

ジブンヲカンジョウニ入レズニ

ヨクミキキシワカリ

ソシテワスレズ

野原ノ松ノ林ノ蔭ノ

小サナ萱ブキノ小屋ニイテ

東ニ病気ノ子供アレバ

行ツテ看病シテヤリ

西ニツカレタ母アレバ

行ツテソノ稲ノ束ヲ負ヒ

南ニ死ニソウナ人アレバ

行ツテコワガラナクテモイイトイイ

北ニケンカヤソショウガアレバ

ツマラナイカラヤメロトイイ

ヒデリノトキハナミダヲナガシ

サムサノナツハオロオロアルキ

ミンナニデクノボウトヨバレ

ホメラレモセズ

クニモサレズ

ソウイウモノニ

ワタシハナリタイ

RESPONSE TEN

March 25, 2011

Hello Anne,

Your Letters from Japan are not only inspiring to read, but full of the Love, Hope, Courage, Kindness and Fortitude that I have known for some time has made you the amazing woman you are.

I have watched the horrors of what has unfolded over there and found no words to respond to you until I was at an AA meeting last Sunday and the subject of "Kindness" was discussed and I realized how profound this word, along with – Honesty, Courage, Acceptance, Willingness and Spirituality – are the principals which bring us complete serenity in our lives.

I see all these principals in your life and the lives of all around you brought on by great tragedy. How similar the alcoholic life of destruction and hopelessness. How wonderful to feel the strength in those around you who bring themselves from the darkness of despair to be born again in the service of others.

You are in a spiritual and humble awakening of the true understanding of who you are. A humble and kind person full of love for others.

I am truly grateful to be a friend.

God bless you and keep you safe,

Dee

P.S. I was with your father for lunch last week and he is well and very thankful that you are well. He told me it was the worst pain he ever went through waiting for news of your safety.

Dee
Baltimore, Maryland USA

RESPONSE ELEVEN

March 26, 2011

Dear Ann,

On Sunday March 20, 2011, our minister at the Unity Church of Greater Portland, Maine, read your detailed account of your current situation in Sendai. There was hardly a dry eye in the sanctuary when she finished. I was so moved with your most uplifting description of how you and others continued demonstration of the goodness in our humanity amidst this peril of nature, that I find few words to describe.

When you wrote "the peeling away of the non-essentials and living with the authenticity of instinct, intuition and caring for the well being of all," I believed you so clearly articulated the true inner desires of our humankind. All of you who are undertaking this tremendous task for survival are absolutely setting invaluable examples for us all.

The press certainly elaborates much about the tremendous physical devastation, but I believe it would inspire you to know that the existing shift, of which you speak, with the resetting of human priorities within each of you have not gone unnoticed and is admired by many in the world outside Japan.

Our church family wants you and others to know that your inner journeys are a beacon of light that remind and encourage us all that now is the time to reclaim building a closer bond between theme and the you, thus creating a world that works better for all. Please know how our prayers and openheartedness connects with your unshakable courage today and each day forward. Thanks again for the sharing of your journey and all the magic that is attached to it. May you have peace that uplifts you and love that surrounds you always.

Namaste,

Barbara

Barbara Sparrow
Portland, Maine

RESPONSE TWELVE

March 27, 2011

Dearest Anne,

We look forward to your letters! I join with all the others in thanking you for sharing your personal experience and innermost thoughts during the aftermath of the tragic earthquake in Japan. It helped put things in perspective for all those who received your message of hope and survival. And amazingly within days your message was being transmitted around the world via the internet, TV, and by word of mouth with praise and gratitude from those who read your gifted words of love and hope.

The acknowledgments keep coming, and the one received yesterday is by far the most beautiful since it includes music "In the Light of Love" by Miten & Deva Premal as a Tribute to Japan, with your letter #1 at the end of the recording. You have friends all over the globe, Anne!

Yours is not a "voice in the wilderness" – your words are reaching a lot of people!

With love & blessings,

Rose

Rose Galuska
Carnegie, Pennsylvania USA

RESPONSE THIRTEEN

March 28th, 2011

On Watching Japan

On the way to visiting my family in Thailand, I often travel on Japan Airlines and stop at Narita airport. Thus Japan is a part of going home for me. In studying Asian culture and modern development, I have read much about life in Japan so felt a kinship with her people. I had respect for their education system, public healthcare system (the best in the world) and the high quality of public transportation was enviable. So to watch such organization and well thought out systems turn to piles of splinters filled me with compassion. Astonishing really to see such an exemplary example of modern living so easily destroyed. Yet how familiar it was to the precariousness of my home in earthquake country here in the Bay Area.

Natural disasters will strike. We know that. We also know that the human population is such that we are densely packed everywhere especially in coastal regions. We know that these densely packed regions are built to resist nature not flow with it, but there is only so much resistance we can build into concrete structures. When natural forces overcome them, the washing away of entire cities has the haunting inevitability of a Greek tragedy. Add to that the even greater hubris of nuclear power plants sitting on unstable fault lines and it is all too clear what a folly our manmade systems are. Thus I felt that Japan was bearing such suffering for all of us really.

When the shelter in place orders were given for those within 20 miles of the broken nuclear power plant, I felt trapped. Looking around the house I wondered if we would have enough food for the length of time it was going to take for the Japanese people to weather this ordeal. Would they have clean water? Clean food? Not likely. What was this karma Japan had with radiation? I felt this power plant disaster would render the country a closed nation. We would want nothing to do with Japan if that would keep the disaster from affecting our lives. These thoughts haunted me for days.

I searched the faces of others in my day to day travels looking for the shell shocked gravity I felt at this folding up of a country. I couldn't quite trust myself not to break into a rant at the slightest opening, with clients, with other Asian faces. I tried to hold the story lightly, but it only made me feel more isolated. At home my partner and brother-in-law, tuned into CNN keeping me updated with breaking news. I joined them, subjecting myself to the fever of impending nuclear meltdown. Where was the transformation in this story? Would this just be another terror of the week and then we go back to what we were doing?

Nearly a week after the tsunami, a contact passed along a letter from an American woman in Sendai describing how the people were coping. It was such a beautiful picture of cooperation and neighborly kindness that I took to heart this little bit of humanity in the face of such overwhelming devastation. The writer reported all the things people were doing to make sure everyone had food and water; how she found food left on her doorstep when she came home; how men in green caps walked around checking that everyone was safe; how people said this was just like the old days when everyone helped each other:

http://www.odemagazine.com/blogs/readers_blog/24755/a_letter_from_sendai

That Japan was still able to remember its humanity and the old way of doing things comforted me greatly. In a BBC account of old people sheltering in a school where there were inadequate supplies, an elderly man said "We're okay. We sit together and talk or read. Everyone has the same as everyone else now. Nothing." I was very moved by those sentiments.

The American woman's letter soon popped up elsewhere, on Facebook, passed along in e-mails and now Ode Magazine *(which since became odewire.com)* hosts her ongoing letters on their blog, so much do her accounts help to heal the overwhelm. (Look for her name in the byline: Anne Thomas):

http://www.odemagazine.com/blogs/readers_blog

She spoke so directly and so articulately to my search for transformation that I offer her words, from the closing paragraph of her first letter, rather than paraphrase her:

"Somehow at this time I realize from direct experience that there is indeed an enormous Cosmic evolutionary step that is occurring all over the world right at this moment. And somehow as I experience the events happening now in Japan, I can feel my heart opening very wide. My brother asked me if I felt so small because of all that is happening. I don't. Rather, I feel as part of something happening that is much larger than myself. This wave of birthing (worldwide) is hard, and yet magnificent."

. . .

How amazing that she spoke of a Cosmic shift, a worldwide birthing. I knew nothing about this woman, why she was living in Japan, what her life was about, yet she seemed to have tapped into exactly the same vein of thought that I had just discovered using almost the same words. And she was describing her days with such a vulnerability and simple power, that I found not only her words to be a balm and a comfort, but the very idea of words themselves to be a comfort. Here just one woman offering her own experience and observation was enough to bring comfort to so many; it poured into me an intense appreciation for the power of words.

I went about my day looking for places where I could work similar magic with words – to comfort a friend who was having a hard time, or to further a message of compassion, humor or mutual experience. This woman who had become an accidental writer for so many, filling in a needed void, had made my own meandering writer's life meaningful, had reminded me that the observations of one person could be just exactly the medicine the world was looking for. And, that what we did mattered, whether in the simple kindnesses of the events she described or the witnessing and reporting of it.

I took comfort in this cosmic evolution of one corner of the world. When I woke from sleeping, even if just a nap, I felt such a sweetness at still being alive and safe that every day became a gift.

Then I went out to buy cans of food to stock our emergency supplies box.

Amanda Kovattana
San Carlos, California, USA

RESPONSE FOURTEEN

March 31, 2011

Hi Anne,

How are you?

Are you in Sendai or you went back to the U.S.?

I believe that you are still in Sendai and I am writing to you from Iran while reading a text which I think it is written by Anne Thomas.

These are some of the words: "Since my shack is even more worthy of that name, I am now staying at a friend's home. We share supplies like water, food and a kerosene heater. We sleep lined up in one room, eat by candlelight, share stories. It is warm, friendly, and beautiful. "

I should say that your essay has been tweeted several times and I also spread it through the Facebook since I think people need to read it specially those who always see the bad sides.

Thank you for the nice job.

Regards,

Amin

Amin Vakhshouri
Tehran, Iran

RESPONSE FIFTEEN

April 1, 2011

Dear Anne,

I am so glad to hear you have decided on a new apartment. I guess you are relieved at least. If you need an extra hand, please let me know I can help you out.

I have been having very tiring weeks since this Tuesday. Every day I went to Yamaya Okino Branch which is one of the biggest store in Sendai. Many messy and muddy cans and bottles from Tsunami are delivered to that store and we wash, brush, and wipe them one by one. Of course we all dress like fishermen (wearing long vinyl aprons and long rubber boots!) and stand all day outside. My body and hands are super COLD and it ends at 6 o'clock every day. Today was the last day of this week and I and some co-workers stopped by a BBQ place and had some drinks and meat. I am SOOOOOOOOOOooo exhausted.

But this is also SOMETHING I can do for this tragedy. Yamaya lost lots of money because of Tsunami and some stores are completely destroyed and nothing is there. At least, I am paid for this job.

Since I have pain all over my body, I will relax this weekend and I will visit the city hall on Sunday if I have energy.

Anyway, so glad to hear your news. Yes, only good things will come up for us from now on!!!

Love,

Junko

Junko Nakano
Sendai, Japan

RESPONSE SIXTEEN

April 4, 2011

Hi Anne,

It is great to hear from you, and thank you sooo much for your consideration.

My family and I have begun to step forward. My dad is so strong in getting himself back from depression. I'm so proud of him. Watching him this close makes me want to support him as much as I can and more than before. I don't think he is expecting anything from me, but I feel that I gotta just live my own life and have my own family eventually. I hope this wish comes true.

Well, I'm with my family now and I'm going to Utsunomiya this Thursday at the earliest to start job hunting.

I'm not sure where my family is going to live and neither am I, but I will keep you updated.

Please let me know your new address.

I hope to meet you when we get more settled!

Love and a smile to you,
Sachi

Sachie Manome
Watari, Miyagi, Japan

RESPONSE SEVENTEEN

April 5, 2011

Dear Anne san,

I am reading your report on the latest situation in Sendai and people, and am very impressed. On 15 Mar, I went to Bangkok for a short stay to meet my friend. The flight from Haneda was fully occupied by foreigners who were trying to evacuate from Japan as quickly as possible.

In Bangkok, I saw lots of Thai people's campaign, students in particular, to support people in Tohoku area. They say, "Japan supported us best whenever we were in problem, particularly at the time of Sumatra Tsunami, therefore, we wish to do something for them."

Anne san, one good news is that Postal cargo deliveries to Sendai have been reopened, although they said no guarantee when the cargo can be delivered. One cargo is maximum of 30Kg, so, I can send you something you or your friends need, perishable products are not possible though. Please do not hesitate to let me know what I should send. Naturally I will let other Sathi members cooperate likewise.

Ganbattekudasai

Kashikuma

Shoichi Kashikuma
Tokyo, Japan

RESPONSE EIGHTEEN

April 10, 2011

Dear friends,

This message has nothing to do with Mother Centers, or maybe it does. I don't know how it is for you, but I have a hard time watching news today. So much going on and all is shown in such a 'technical' way. What happens during all that to human beings in Libya, Japan, Ivory Coast, how do they manage to eat, sleep, bath, take care of the old and young? That story, what you don't hear in the news, is described in the letters that my friend Anne has written. She is from the USA originally, but has lived in Sendai for over 20 years now where she works as a teacher. Since the letters have such beauty and wisdom to them, I asked if I can pass them on. She answered "Yes, please pass them on. The world is my family now."

So in attachment please find messages with love, from your 'aunt' Anne in Japan.

Marieke

Marieke Geldermalsen
Amsterdam, The Netherlands

RESPONSE NINETEEN

April 16, 2011

I was so honoured to read your most recent letter, it is very fun to be part of your communicative outreach.

There is no issue with what you said, Yuki's dad is retired. He is 76 and was never a firefighter. He was a communications operator for the Japanese ships monitoring the fishing industry, kind of like the coast guard. When he retired he became a member of the mayors office, like a town council, a representative for the area.

When the quake struck he assumed position as a fire fighter, he boarded the fire trucks, sans experience, and shooed the community to safety, and then (again at 76) acted as a firefighter in the rescue missions for one month – again with not one day off. This is why he is a hero, because he is not a firefighter, but a normal man – acting as one, acting above it.

You also know the rules in Japan. If you are not a firefighter there is no way you could enter this field, unless you as a devoted human as he is. He saw a need and became more than he was. There was no way he would not resume this role. Should be a contender for the CCN heroes they have each year – really.

They are living at their home without running water – and would have it no other way. They may be needed.

:)

Steve

Steve Pellerine
Ras Al Khaimah
United Arab Emirates

RESPONSE TWENTY

April 24, 2011

Anne:

I am a close friend of Georgiana's and she has been nice enough to share your amazing and informative letters with us since first contacting you.

It seems you have other things to do than read e-mails from strangers so I was reluctant to write, but now I feel I must. I think you should know there are a whole group of us — George's book club, friends and family — who are connected to you in so many ways and who hope and pray for you and the residents of Japan every day. Your letters are simply amazing and I hope you put them together in a book some day for the ages, when life settles down, which I know it will. In spite of having experienced earthquakes here in Northern California, were it not for your letters I do not believe we would have any way to imagine the plight of the Japanese people and the incredible disruption and loss of normality. You have so well depicted the inner feelings and outward turmoil of this wretched disruption to your lives.

Let me send my thanks for sharing these bits and pieces of the human response, heroism and strength, and even the human weaknesses — all that I believe binds us all together in the human race. I went to the San Francisco Symphony a few weeks ago after the first wave of the tsunami. Two of the violinists, who come from Japan spoke about the tragedy and asked for people to help through the Red Cross and the Japanese Cultural Assn. They began the program with the Japanese National Anthem. It was very moving. (I was surprised to find the anthem sounds like music from Madame

Butterfly ... I think Puccini must have borrowed!) I spoke with them in the lobby and they were so gracious and frightened for their people. As you might imagine, most everyone there felt compelled to help. I hope you will let Georgiana know if there is any way we can assist.

Warmest thoughts,

Nancy

Nancy Weiner
San Jose, California

RESPONSE TWENTY-ONE

May 22, 2011

Dear Anne,

Please know that you have been in my thoughts everyday since we spoke with you. Your letters have been an inspiration to me in so many ways. Because you have been through so much, I have not written that I fell and broke my hip last September and have had a slow recovery due to back complications. After reading your letters, my thoughts have often gone to those who were injured and to those who have to care for them under such unbelievably difficult circumstances. My own experience has made me more sensitive to people who have physical limitations and opened my eyes to so much more around me. It has been so good for me to hear how courageous people are in confronting the challenges in their lives after the quake and tsunami. The Japanese people are rare indeed. We have much to learn from them and you are helping us do that. I recently heard a program on NPR about Eliza Scidmore, the writer for National Geographic who wrote about the terrible earthquake in Japan in the late 1800's and then later contributed to the planting of cherry trees in Washington, D.C. She made me think of you as another American woman who writes about Japan.

My heart was full when I read your comments about living in silence and experiencing your new life in your new apartment. It is a life that is so foreign to most of us who live in a society that constantly bombards us with outside noise and information. It almost feels like a necessity sometimes and then it is a relief when we turn it off. Even though I am not able to return to yoga yet, the breathing exercises are a great help to me. I have tried to imagine you living as you described "in the moment." It seems it is much more profound than the "in the moment" living of popular culture.

Your writing is so beautiful. Thank you for sharing yourself through your letters. I wish I could be half as eloquent in letting you know how much you mean to me.

Love, Georgiana

Georgiana Flaherty
San Jose, California

RESPONSE TWENTY-TWO

May 30, 2011

I think of you and all Japanese people very often. I am very grateful for all your strength and kindness for sharing with us a little bit of what these people really are.

Samira C. V. Morais Martins

Brasilia, Brazil

RESPONSE TWENTY-THREE

June 2, 2011

Dear Anne,

It is an honor and a pleasure to "talk" with you directly after so many weeks of reading (and helping my students to present orally) your beautifully written letters.

I send good wishes as you begin, in a sense, a new life.

Nancy

Nancy Greenaway
Block Island, Rhode Island USA

RESPONSE TWENTY-FOUR

June 6, 2011

ai-je bien compris? Tu vas peut-etre pouvoir mettre tes ecrits sur cd et pourquoi pas sous forme de livre? Tes amies pensent que tu as bien parlé de cette effroyable expérience du tremblement de terre et du tsunami de la devastation et de l'energie de tout un chacu pour se reconstruire personnelement et dans toute la société. C'est dans ces périodes tragiques que revient la solidarité, la compassion pour les plus démunis. quand la vie est tranquille les egoismes ont la vie dure et rien n'est remis en cause qui pourrait gener le confort des gens qui ne manquent de rien. Je ne sais pas comment faire pour envoyer un don à tes associations mais j'ai pu aller à un tres beau concert pour le japon c'etait de la musique classique.

Translation:

Have I understood correctly? Possibly you will put your writing on a CD and why not into a book, too? Your friends feel that you have spoken well concerning this horrendous experience of the earthquake and tsunami, of the devastation, and of the energy that everyone is pouring forth to reconstruct, not only personally, but within the entire society also. It is in times of great tragedy that solidarity and compassion for the least of us are reborn. When life is calm and peaceful, narcissists have a difficult time, and nothing that might disrupt the comforts of those who have everything is ever questioned.

I have no idea how to send a donation to an association to help the Japanese, but I was able to attend a beautiful concert for the benefit of Japan. It was classical music.

Love,

Ma Jo

MariJosé Jaquemet
Paris, France

RESPONSE TWENTY-FIVE

June 17, 2011

Hi, Anne,

How have you been?

I went to Minami-sanriku on Wednesday with a couple from Perugia, Italy and their friend.

They kindly donated two machines called skywater which can produce water from vapour in the air to Minami-sanriku.

http://www.skywater.it/english/home_en.html

They placed one machine at an elementary school called Isakimae Elementary school in Utatsu area.

The school used to be used as a place for dead bodies after Tsunami.

The other machine was placed at Hotel Kanyo which has been used as a shelter since 11th March.

500 people used to live there, but now only 100 live there. But during day time still 500 people spend their time at the hotel as the place can get water and food.

To my great surprise, Minami-sanriku area still does not have water supply!

The area looks like war fields with only dusty roads, and piles of gabage, broken buildings.

On 19th, I am going to go to Higashi Matsuhima with students from FSU to attend Cooking Activity for people in shelters.

I will talk to you soon.

Take care.

Lots of Love & Light,
Kumiko

Kumiko Suganami
Sendai, Japan

Past
Perfect

TWO PERSPECTIVES · ONE TRUTH

Excerpts from a Letter & Times Past

Letters from the Ground to the Heart closes with an extraordinary letter, a treasured keepsake of Anne Thomas and her family. The following extrapolation on portions of the Foreword puts this letter in its full and proper context.

. . .

The following excerpts are taken from a letter written by Anne's late Uncle, Henry "Had" Brown over the course of several days in October, 1945. Ironically, Had also chronicled events in and around the environs of Sendai, Japan to family and friends following disaster, albeit one that was manmade vs. natural – while on leave as an officer in the U.S. Navy at the close of World War II.

It is doubly ironic, if not uncanny that the observations of Anne and her Uncle Had bracket the exact period of time during which nuclear events forever changed, and are yet again reshaping both Japan and our entire world. However and rather than delving into such bleak matters, their writings ultimately offer the prospect of hope.

Where Anne's writing focuses more on the people of Japan, and both chronicle aspects of Japan's culture; Had was clearly fascinated by its natural beauty. And while each writes from distinctly different vantage points, their two perspectives are separated only by time and circumstances. Both reveal one, consummate and powerfully enduring truth: that the timeless, mystical nature of Japan is inextricably intertwined with the kind spirit, patience and generosity of its people – call it their 'cultural fortitude,' which the Japanese seem somehow hardwired to share not only with each other, but especially and instinctively in times of extreme challenge with those around them, as well.

Much of the once pristine, rural Japan that so captivated Had Brown may no longer be recognizable as such – not as any result of recent events, rather and due simply to the burgeoning growth that made Japan a major economic force in the latter half of the twentieth century. Nonetheless, many of Had's observations of an old world Japan still ring true.

The spectacles Had evokes in the mind's eye are stunning. It is as though at times one is actually meandering somewhere rather than reading – and perhaps most remarkably, not in Japan, but amid the more unspoiled regions of the United States. In one moment the Japanese countryside that Had brings alive, and its natural waterways that seem to be everywhere conjure rural New England, its hills and valleys draped in the splendor of Fall. While at other times, one could be trekking along a narrow, mountainous pass – west of the Rockies, that is.

Then there are the casual references that evidence being on the very cusp, the earliest dawn of the Technology Age, and a (then) economy in which 'a hundred dollars' meant something closer to 'a million' in today's vernacular – all of which serve to make Had's letter a fascinating portal to a time and world that would be lost forever, were it not for the written word.

At once astonishing and most heartening is that in the course of an off-duty tour, a mere two months after atomic bombs decimated Nagasaki and Hiroshima, Had and his fellow travelers, officers from various branches of the U.S. military one and all, encountered not one word nor hint of bitterness, let alone anger or hatred from the Japanese populace – or from their many, gracious, Japanese hosts along the way.

Here then are excerpts transcribed from the original, reformatted to fit these pages.

HENRY "HAD" BROWN · EXCERPTS FROM A LETTER

October 23, 1945 *(and as compiled over several weeks preceding)*

Dear People:

We set out from Sendai on the 5th – in two jeeps and a pair of trailers laden with gasoline, chow and personal effects, until the springs bent double. When you travel in this country you must count on carrying all your necessities with you.

By great fortune, the gentle rains of the previous two days had stopped overnight and left the air clear as it always is after rain, as though it had been not only washed but scrubbed. The sun was glorious, just warm enough to make driving comfortable.

The countryside was beautiful as always – neat fields of beans and yellow rice; houses of weathered wood or soft white stucco tucked snugly, each one in its own little grove of dark green trees; forested mountains flecked with the first touches of fall; and everywhere streams rushing with the burden of the rains just ceased. New Yorkers catching their first glimpse of the green Mountains couldn't have been more enthusiastic than we were. We craned our necks and pointed out especially attractive scenes for all the morning and after that we just looked, as if we could never have our fill.

In one small city the people were out in force. They lined the main street three and four deep, as though waiting for a parade, and every one was dressed in his best. I would have given a hundred dollars for a movie camera and some rolls of Kodachrome. The men were drab in uniforms or nondescript mufti, as usual, but lost of the women were wearing mompei with bold line patterns of great checks of pastel colors, while the kids... ! Every one of them under six years were clad in a kimono that fairly shrieked. We never saw such bright colors, or so many of them tied together. Red, orange, yellow, white, blue, purple, positively vibrating, there were so intense, were splashed in floral designs or sewn together in great squares the size of your palm. They alone would have kept a child warm. Just to be sure, though, many of the babies were muffled in little quilted coats of the same gaudy materials and some wore hats of red or orange. It was a sight to remember, literally dazzling as the people moved to and fro.

We passed through several small cities that had not been touched by bombs. The main streets were much like those of small cities at home, with paved streets, sidewalks, stone or concrete stores, banks and office buildings, trolley tracks and so on. Americans were few in the cities and the Japanese didn't pay any attention to us. Out in the villages it was different. Little kids ran to the roadside and threw up both hands and hollered as we passed, and mothers grabbed their youngsters and hustled them indoors to peek at us.

The drive was perfectly marvelous and believe me, we marveled. We traveled at first through a countryside very much like what I imagine England to be, with gently rolling fields of rice and green squares of beans and peanuts, with orchards, and thatched houses set close in little groves. Then the land grew steeper. Hills rose beside us and turned into young mountains thick with cherry, birch and evergreens and clothed in a gentle gray fog that drifted through the valleys. It was beautiful with a quiet, moving beauty such as would never be found in bold sunlight. We stared and stared. Then we came to a lake, Inawashiro-ko (you can find it right in the middle of Honshu), with huge headlands shouldering out of the mist and little waves splashing almost onto our jeeps as we drove around the shore. We crossed another mountain pass gay with leaves turning and about to turn, and arrived at Wakamatsu. This is a large city, as big as Sendai, which came unscathed through the war. As we drove through the streets (paved) we spied many little shops, which we hoped to investigate on the morrow.

October 8

Our quarters are in a hotel in a spot so picturesque that one could not imagine it. It is as if the prettiest parts of New Hope *(Pennsylvania)* had found their way into an old-fashioned Japanese painting. A torrent sweeps down a narrow gorge between hills so high their forested tops are lost in the mists which drift above the valley. A tiny village of stone and wood clings to the sides of the gorge wherever there is a ledge to place the foundations of the houses on. Tiny narrow streets wind through it, and two wooden bridges hang above the torrent. Our hotel used to cater to the elite among tourists. We leave our shoes at the door, don woven slippers that are far too small, and shuffle about the glistening floors. The house is built on several different levels, all the rooms with sliding paper doors, all the woodwork beautifully polished. Our room is right beside the stream and a foot above it. The sound of rushing water is soothing as rain and gentle wind.

We all wait for the General and all sit down at the table together. Each place is set on a square tray of brilliant red lacquer, and the condiments and sauces are put out in the middle of the table where everybody reaches for them unembarrassed. Japanese maids wait on us. The officers kid them in English and hybrid Japanese and they kid right back.

After supper the houseman appears to make our beds. Yes, of course the room is floored with mats, straw ones two or three inches thick, which are immaculate. It is défendu to wear anything but socks on your feet inside the bedroom door.

October 9

They said there was a landslide in the road between Wakamatsu and Niigata that had not yet been repaired, so we arranged to make the journey by train. It was wonderful to let your eyes rove over the carriage. The scene outside was as gorgeous as the one inside was varied. We traveled through the mountains down a valley where we lost site of the water only as we passed through the tunnels that bespeckled our route. I regretted to see evening come, for the countryside had no lights as our does and when the sun set the outside world disappeared into an opaque black void. Inside the car two feeble bulbs of some ten watts a piece provided our sole illumination. People lost animation. They began to look tired and grubby. Only a quartet of schoolboys behind us continued to talk, their conversation growing noisier as the car emptied. It was very much like the Sunday evening Trenton local.

Yesterday Smith (my Chief) and I drove south to Takada in off-and-on weather, a bit of sun and a spurt of rain but mostly just clouds. As Oliver, our philosopher, says, "It isn't difficult to see why Japanese painting is that way. Everything begins in nothing and ends in nothing." So it was yesterday. Japan in the rain is a faery place, all soft white mists and grotesque evergreens, neat cottages of yellow earth and foot-thick thatch all green with moss, a land of yellow rice fields and tiny lanes hidden between great walls of rice hung up to dry. The rain fell in soft, small drops, dimming the prospect and reducing every color to a low, smooth blend of tones which faded into the vapor rising from the rivers; behind floated the mists, and over them one could catch a glimpse of mountains rearing without weight and almost without form until they were themselves lost in drifting clouds. So it was yesterday, mystically beautiful, and chilly as the outer circle of Orcus. In can get awfully uncomfortable in this neighborhood without becoming particularly cold. We had on sweaters and combat jackets, but it took a poncho on top of that to keep out the wind. Ponchos are a great invention.

The part of our path that led along the seaside was as picturesque as any place I have seen. The road was just a one-lane way scraped out of the side of a mountain escarpment. It would wind in and out like a living contour line. Below us the cliffs dropped sheer to the narrowest of beaches where the railroad ran behind the sea wall and waves tumbled to the shore. Off the rocky points there would be a scattering of grotesquely carved rocks and once on a particularly ragged and precipitous specimen of these bits of lava I glimpsed a white torii set between two dark pine trees. This land is full of classical touches. It is difficult to decide whether it is more like Greece or England – the storybook countries, I mean. Some day I should like to come back with a speaking knowledge of Japanese and a bicycle.

The remainder of our trip was uneventful. We got back to Sendai yesterday. Since we can't get orders to go home, we feel we may as well see as much of this country as we can.

This is just a stopgap note. I hope to be able to reply to all your letters in time. Meanwhile, thanks an awful lot for all of them.

Love,

Had

HOW
TO HELP

How You can Help Survivors of the Tohoku (aka) Great East Japan Earthquake & Tsunami

Whether you purchased *Letters from the Ground to the Heart – Beauty Amid Destruction* or received it as a gift, we hope that you continue to benefit by its insights. If you enjoy this book, please share the awareness of it with as many others as possible.

The international news media that brought Japan's tragic events of March 2011 to the attention of the world has long since gone home, while many in Japan still *no longer have* homes.

Your help is yet badly needed – and will be, for some time to come.

Proceeds after expenses from sales of *Letters from the Ground to the Heart* go directly to assist survivors of the devastating earthquake and tsunami of March 11, 2011. Additional copies of *'Letters'* may also be purchased at finer book sellers, or online at:

www.lulu.com
www.amazon.com
www.barnesandnoble.com

You can also find additional information and ways to donate at:

www.anneinjapan.com
www.lettersfromthegroundtotheheart.com

However you choose to give, your generous contributions will help fund earthquake and tsunami relief efforts in Japan in ways that matter most – *on the ground and from the heart.*

...

Funds are distributed under the kind auspices of our host non profit organization, Block Island Ecumenical Ministries (BIEM), Inc.

ACKNOWLEDGEMENTS

Infinite gratitude to Izumi and her mother,
who for five long weeks cared for me
as a family member, despite having
major concerns of their own.

Also, deep admiration for Imai Sensei,
who ceaselessly serves the homeless,
giving all and keeping nothing for himself.

And of course, deep appreciation
to Brian Penry for his idealism, expertise,
and hard work, without which this project
would never have come to fruition.

About The Author and Editor of
Letters from the Ground to the Heart

Anne Thomas teaches English in Sendai Japan, her home of 22 years. Formerly an Associate Professor at Shokei Women's College for 15 years, she currently teaches at Miyagi Women's University, as well as private classes.

Originally from Maryland, Anne received her BA in Art from the University of Rhode Island, her Masters in Education from George Washington University, and her Certification to Teach English as a Foreign Language from International House, London.

Prior to settling in Japan, Anne traveled extensively throughout virtually every continent and corner of the globe for 15 years, during which she taught for extended periods in Spain, Morocco and Indonesia.

Letters from the Ground to the Heart – Beauty Amid Destruction is her first English language book.

...

Brian Penry edited and wrote the Foreword for *Letters from the Ground to the Heart – Beauty Amid Destruction,* as well as art directing and designing its cover and text.

A Founding Member of the Creating WE Institute, Brian also contributed to the Institute's (2009) Amazon Best Seller, *42 Rules for Creating WE* – art directing its cover design, as well.

A designer, illustrator, writer and editor since 1972, his focus is on branding and writing for the arts & entertainment, non profit organizations and others – including cause-related initiatives in Sub-Saharan Africa and elsewhere. He lives and works in Guilford, Connecticut, USA.